Other Works by Marguerite Duras
Published by Grove Press

Destroy, She Said

Four Novels
(The Afternoon of Mr. Andesmas;
10:30 On a Summer Night;
Moderato Cantabile;
The Square)

Hiroshima Mon Amour

The Ravishing of Lol Stein

# India Song

MARGUERITE
DURAS

# India
# Song

Translated by
BARBARA BRAY

Grove Press, Inc.
New York

*India Song* was written in August, 1972,
at the request of Peter Hall,
director of the National Theatre, London.

# India Song

# Characters

ANNE-MARIE STRETTER

THE BEGGAR WOMAN

MICHAEL RICHARDSON

THE YOUNG ATTACHÉ (not named)

THE STRETTERS' GUEST (not named)

GEORGE CRAWN

THE FRENCH VICE-CONSUL IN LAHORE (not named)

FIRST SERVANT

SECOND SERVANT

10 women extras

10 men extras

2 WOMEN'S VOICES

2 MEN'S VOICES

# General Remarks

The names of Indian towns, rivers, states, and seas are used here primarily in a musical sense.

All references to physical, human, or political geography are incorrect:

You can't drive from Calcutta to the estuary of the Ganges in an afternoon. Nor to Nepal.

The "Prince of Wales" hotel is not on an island in the Delta, but in Colombo.

And New Delhi, not Calcutta, is the administrative capital of India.

And so on.

The characters in the story have been taken out of a book called *The Vice-consul* and projected into new narrative regions. So it is not possible to relate them back to the book and see *India Song* as a film or theatre adaptation of *The Vice-consul*. Even where a whole episode is taken over from the book, its insertion into the new narrative means that it has to be read, seen, differently.

In fact, *India Song* follows on from *The Woman of the Ganges*. If *The Woman of the Ganges* hadn't been written, neither would *India Song*. The fact that it goes into and reveals an unexplored area of *The Vice-consul* wouldn't have been a sufficient reason.

What was a sufficient reason was the discovery, in *The Woman of the Ganges*, of the *means* of exploration, revelation: the voices external to the narrative. This discovery made it possible to let the narrative be forgotten and put at the disposal of memories other than that of the author: memories which might remember, in the same way, any other love story. Memories that distort. That create.

Some voices from *The Woman of the Ganges* have been used here. And even some of their words.

That is about all that can be said.

As far as I know, no "India Song" yet exists. When it has been written, the author will make it available and it should be used for all performances of *India Song* in France and elsewhere.

If by any chance *India Song* were performed in France, there should be no public dress rehearsal. This does not apply to other countries.

# I

# Notes on Voices 1 and 2

VOICES 1 and 2 are women's voices. Young.

They are linked together by a love story.

Sometimes they speak of this love, their own. Most of the time they speak of another love, another story. But this other story leads us back to theirs. And vice versa.

Unlike the men's voices—VOICES 3 and 4, which don't come in until the end of the narrative—the women's voices are tinged with madness. Their sweetness is pernicious. Their memory of the love story is illogical, anarchic. Most of the time they are in a state of transport, a delirium, at once calm and feverish. VOICE 1 is consumed with the story of ANNE-MARIE STRETTER. VOICE 2 is consumed with its passion for VOICE 1.

They should always be heard with perfect clarity,

but the level varies according to what they are saying. They are most immediately present when they veer toward their own story—that is, when, in the course of a perpetual shifting process, the love story of *India Song* is juxtaposed with their own. But there is a distinction. When they speak of the story we see unfolding before us, they rediscover it at the same time we do, and so are frightened and perhaps moved by it in the same way we are. But when they speak of their own story, they are always shot through with desire, and we should feel the difference between their two passions. Above all, we should feel the terror of VOICE 2 at the fascination the resuscitated story exerts over VOICE 1. VOICE 1 is in danger of being "lost" in the story of *India Song*, which is in the past, legendary, a model. VOICE 1 is in danger of departing its own life.

The voices are never raised, and their sweetness remains constant.

*Blackout.*

*A tune from between the two wars, "India Song,"
is played slowly on the piano.*

*It is played right through, to cover the time—always
long—that it takes the audience, or the reader, to
emerge from the ordinary world they are in when the
performance, or the book, begins.*

*"India Song" still.*

*Still.*

*And now it ends.*

*Now it is repeated, "farther away" than the first
time, as if it were being played elsewhere.*

*Now it is played at its usual rhythm—blues.*

*The darkness begins to lighten.*

*As the dark slowly disperses, suddenly there are*

*voices. Others besides ourselves were watching, hear-ing, what we thought we alone were watching and hearing. They are women. The voices are slow, sweet. Very close, enclosed like us in this place. And intan-gible, inaccessible.*

VOICE 1: He followed her to India.
VOICE 2: Yes.

*Pause.*

VOICE 2: For he left everything.
   Overnight.
VOICE 1: The night of the dance?
VOICE 2: Yes.

*The light continues to grow. We still hear "India Song." The voices are silent for some time. Then they begin again:*

VOICE 1: Was it she who played the piano?
VOICE 2 (*hesitating*): Yes . . . but he played too . . . It was he who used sometimes, in the evening, to play the tune they played in S. Thala . . .

*Silence.*

*A house in India. Huge. A "white people's" house.*
   *Divans. Armchairs.*
*Furniture of the period of "India Song."*
*A ceiling fan is working, but at nightmare slowness.*

*Net screens over the windows. Beyond, the paths of*
*a large tropical garden. Oleanders. Palm trees.*
*Complete stillness. No wind outside. Inside, dense*
*shadow. Is it the evening? We don't know.*
*Space. Gilt. A piano. Unlit chandeliers. Indoor*
*plants. Nothing moves, nothing except the fan,*
*which moves with nightmare "unreality."*
*The slowness of the voices goes with the very slow*
*growth of the light; their sweetness matches*
*the poignancy of the setting.*

VOICE 1 (*as if reading*): "Michael Richardson was en-
gaged to a girl from S. Thala. Lola Valérie Stein.
They were to have been married in the autumn.
Then there was the dance.
The dance at S. Thala . . ."

*Silence.*

VOICE 2: She arrived at the dance late . . . in the mid-
dle of the night . . .
VOICE 1: Yes . . . *dressed in black* . . .
What love, at the dance . . .
What desire . . .

*Silence.*

*As the light grows we see, set in this colonial décor,*
*presences. There were people there all the time.*
*They are behind either a row of plants, or a fine net*
*screen, or a transparent blind, or smoke from*

*perfume burners—something which makes the
second part of the space explored less easily
visible.*

*Lying on a divan, long, slender, almost thin, is a
woman dressed in black.*

*Sitting close to her is a man, also dressed in black.*

*Away from the lovers there is another man in black.*
    *(One of the men is smoking a cigarette—is that
what made us sense there were people there?)*

VOICE 1 *discovers—after we do—the presence of
the woman in black.*

VOICE 1 (*tense, low*): Anne-Marie Stretter . . .

*It is as if* VOICE 2 *had not heard.*

VOICE 2 (*low*): How pale you are . . . what are you
frightened of . . .

*No answer.*
*Silence.*

*The three people seem struck by a deathly stillness.*
*"India Song" has stopped.*
*The voices grow lower, to match the deathliness of
the scene.*

VOICE 2: After she died, he left India . . .

*Silence.*

*That was said all in one breath, as if recited slowly.*
*So the woman in black, there in front of us, is dead.*
*The light is now steady, somber.*
*Silence everywhere.*
*Near and far.*
*The voices are full of pain. Their memory, which*
*was gone, is coming back. But they are as sweet,*
*as gentle as before.*

VOICE 2: She's buried in the English cemetery . . .

*Pause.*

VOICE 1: . . . she died there?
VOICE 2: In the islands. (*Hesitates.*) One night. Found
dead.

*Silence.*

*"India Song" again, slow, far away.*
*At first we don't see the movement, the beginnings*
*of movement. But it begins exactly on the first*
*note of "India Song."*
*The woman in black and the man sitting near her*
*begin to stir. Emerge from death. Their foot-*
*steps make no sound.*
*They are standing up.*
*They are close together.*
*What are they doing?*
*They are dancing.*

*Dancing. We only realize it when they are already dancing.*

*They go on, slowly, dancing.*

*When* VOICE 1 *speaks they have been dancing for some time.*

VOICE 1 *is gradually remembering.*

VOICE 1: The French Embassy in India . . .
VOICE 2: Yes.

*Pause.*

VOICE 1: That murmur? The Ganges?
VOICE 2: Yes.

*Pause.*

VOICE 1: That light?
VOICE 2: The monsoon.
VOICE 1: . . . no wind . . .
VOICE 2 (*continues*): . . . it will break over Bengal . . .
VOICE 1: The dust?
VOICE 2: The middle of Calcutta.

*Silence.*

VOICE 1: Isn't there a smell of flowers?
VOICE 2: Leprosy.

*Silence.*

*They are still dancing to "India Song."*
*They are dancing. But it needs to be said.*
(*As if otherwise it weren't sure. And so that the
image and the voices coincide, touch.*)

VOICE 2: They're dancing.

*Silence.*

VOICE 2: In the evening they used to dance.

*Silence.*

*They dance.*
*So close they are one.*
*"India Song" fades in the distance.*
*They are merged together in the dance, almost
motionless.*
*Now quite motionless.*

VOICE 2: Why are you crying?

*No answer.*

*Silence.*

*No more music.*
*A murmur in the distance. Then it stops. Other
murmurs.*
*They, the man and woman, are still motionless in
the silence hemmed in by sound.*

*Fixed. Arrested.*
*It lasts a long while.*
*Over the fixed couple:*

VOICE 2: I love you so much I can't see any more,
    can't hear . . .
        . . . can't live . . .

*No answer.*

*Silence.*

*"India Song" comes back from far away. Slowly*
    *the couple unfreeze, come back to life.*
*Sound increases behind the music: the sound of*
    *Calcutta: a loud, a great murmur. All around,*
    *various other sounds. The regular cries of*
    *merchants. Dogs. Shouts in the distance.*
*As the sound outside increases, the sky in the*
    *garden becomes overcast. Murky light. No*
    *wind.*

*Silence.*

*The couple separate and turn toward the garden.*
    *They look out at it, motionless.*
*The second man sitting there also begins to look*
    *out at the garden.*
*The light grows still murkier.*
*The sound of Calcutta ceases.*
*Waiting.*

*Waiting. It is almost dark.*
*Suddenly the waiting is over:*
*The noise of the rain.*
*A cool, slaking noise.*
*It is raining over Bengal.*
*The rain cannot be seen. Only heard. As if it were*
    *raining everywhere except in the garden, deleted*
    *from life.*
*Everyone looks at the sound of the rain.*

VOICE 2 (*scarcely voiced*): It's raining over Bengal  . . .
VOICE 1: An ocean  . . .

*Silence.*

*Cries in the distance, of joy, shouts in Hindustani,*
    *the unknown language.*
*The light gradually returns.*
*The rain, the noise, very loud for a few seconds.*
*It grows less. Isolated shouts and laughter are heard*
    *more clearly through the sound of the rain.*
*The light continues to grow stronger.*
*Suddenly, clearer, nearer cries—a woman's. Her*
    *laughter.*

VOICE 1: Someone's shouting  . . .  a woman  . . .
VOICE 2: What?
VOICE 1: Disconnected words.
    She's laughing.
VOICE 2: A beggar.

*Pause.*

VOICE 1: Mad?
VOICE 2: Yes . . .

> *In the garden paths, sun after the rain. Moving*
> *sunlight. Patches of light, gray, pale.*
> *Still the shouting and laughter of the* BEGGAR
> WOMAN.

VOICE 1: Oh yes . . . I remember. She goes by the
banks of the rivers . . . is she from Burma?
VOICE 2: Yes.

> *While the voices speak of the beggar, the three*
> *people move, leave the room by side doors.*

VOICE 2: She's not Indian.
She comes from Savannakhet.
Born there.
VOICE 1: Ah yes . . . yes . . .
One day . . . she's been walking ten years, and
one day, there in front of her, the Ganges?
VOICE 2: Yes.
And there she stops.
VOICE 1: Yes . . .

> *The three people have disappeared. The place is*
> *empty.*
> *Someone speaking, almost shouting, in the distance,*
> *in a soft-sounding language, Laotian.*

VOICE 1 (*after a pause*): Twelve children die while
she's walking to Bengal . . . ?

VOICE 2: Yes. She leaves them. Sells them. Forgets them. (*Pause.*) On the way to Bengal, becomes barren.

*The three people reach the garden and stroll slowly through the cool after the rain, moving through the patches of sunlight. In the distance, the shouting of the* BEGGAR WOMAN, *still. Suddenly, in the shouting, the word* SAVANNAKHET.
*The voices halt briefly. Then resume:*

VOICE 1: Savannakhet—Laos?
VOICE 2: Yes. (*Pause.*) Seventeen . . . she's pregnant, she's seventeen . . . (*Pause.*) She's turned out by her mother, goes away. (*Pause.*) She asks the way to get lost. Remember?
No one knows.
VOICE 1 (*pause*): Yes.
One day, she's been walking ten years, and one day: Calcutta, there in front of her.
She stays.

*Silence.*

VOICE 2: She's there on the banks of the Ganges, under the trees. She has forgotten.

*Silence.*

*The three people go out of the garden.*
*Movements of light, monsoon, in the empty garden.*

*The song of the beggar—"song of Savannakhet"*
     *—in the distance.*
(VOICE 2 *is informative, calm, gentle.*)

VOICE 2: Lepers burst like sacks of dust, you know.
VOICE 1: Don't suffer?
VOICE 2: No. Not a thing.
     Laugh.

                                   *Silence.*

VOICE 2: They were there together, in Calcutta. The
white woman and the other. During the same years.

*The voices are silent.*
*A distant part of the garden, so far very dark, as if*
     *neglected by the lighting, gradually becomes*
     *visible. It is revealed by spotlights—extremely*
     *slowly, but regularly, mathematically.*
*Far away, the song of Savannakhet—coming, going.*
     *Sound of Calcutta, in the distance.*
*The wire netting round a tennis court emerges*
     *from the darkness. Against the wire a woman's*
     *bicycle—red.*
*The place is deserted.*
*The voices recognize these things and are afraid:*

VOICE 1 (*smothered exclamation of fear*): The tennis
courts, deserted . . .
VOICE 2 (*the same*): . . . Anne-Marie Stretter's red
bicycle . . .

*Silence.*

*A man has come into the garden. Tall, thin, dressed
  in white. He walks slowly. His footsteps make
  no sound.*
*He gazes around him at the stillness everywhere.
  Gazes for some time. Tries to see into the house:
  no one there.*
*Now what is he looking at? We don't know at first.
  Then it becomes clear: he's looking at* ANNE-
  MARIE STRETTER's *red bicycle by the deserted
  tennis courts.*
*He goes over to the bicycle. Stops. Hesitates.
  Doesn't go any nearer. Looks, stares at it.*
*(The voices are low, scared.)*

VOICE 2: . . . he comes every night . . .

*Pause.*

VOICE 1: The French Vice-consul in Lahore . . .
VOICE 2: Yes.
         . . . in Calcutta in disgrace . . .

*Silence.*

*Slowly, the man in white moves. He walks. He goes
  along a path. He goes away.*
*Disappears.*
*After he has disappeared, everything remains in
  suspense.*

*Silence. Fear.*
*The song of Savannakhet, in the distance, innocent.*
*Then, two shots.*
*The first makes the light go dim.*
*The second makes it go out.*

*Silence.*

*Blackout.*

*The song of Savannakhet stopped when the shots*
 *were fired. As if they had been aimed at it.*

*Silence.*

*Blackout.*

*The voices are very quiet, terrified.*

VOICE 2: Someone fired a gun under the trees . . . on
the banks of the Ganges . . .

           *Silence.*

VOICE 1: It was a song of Savannakhet . . . ?
VOICE 2: Yes.

           *Silence.*

*By a strictly symmetrical inversion, and without*
 *passing through any intermediate stages, the*

*light becomes the same as it was when the first*
*shot made it go dim.*
*This stands for night.*
*It is night.*
*The place, the stage, is still empty.*
*The only movement—that of the nightmare fan.*
*Time passes over the empty place.*

*Silence.*

*A Hindu servant dressed in white goes by, passing*
*through the drawing rooms of the French Em-*
*bassy.*
*He has gone. Emptiness again.*
*Far away, the song of Savannakhet begins again:*
*the* BEGGAR WOMAN *wasn't killed.*
*The voices are still low, frightened.*

VOICE 1: . . . she's not dead . . .
VOICE 2: Can't die.
VOICE 1 (*scarcely heard*): No . . .

*Silence.*

VOICE 2: She goes hunting at night beside the Ganges.
For food . . .

*No answer.*

*Silence.*

VOICE 1: Where's the one dressed in black?
VOICE 2: Out. Every evening.
  She comes back when it's dark

*Silence.*

*A servant enters, lights a lamp, very faint, in a
    corner of the room. Does various things.*
*Goes away (but remains visible).*
*Comes back.*
*Opens a window.*
*Perhaps he lights some sticks of incense against the
    mosquitoes—in which case the audience will be
    able to smell it.*
*Empties ashtrays.*

VOICE 2: She's back.
  The Embassy's black Lancia has just come through
  the gates.

*Silence.*

*The servant goes out.*
*The place remains empty for a few more seconds,
    and then the woman in black enters the dark-
    ness. She is barefoot. Her hair is loose. She is
    wearing a short wrap of loose black cotton.*
*The scene is very long and slow.*
*Slowly she goes and stands under the nightmare
    fan. Stays there.*
*Puts up her hands and thrusts her hair away from*

*her body in a gesture of exhaustion—someone
stifling from the heat. Then lets her arms fall
down by her sides.*

*Through the opening of the wrap, the white of the
naked body.*

*She freezes. Head thrown back. Gasping for air.
Trying to escape out of the heat.*

*Touching grace of the thin, fragile body.*

*Stays like that, upright, exposed. Offered to the
voices.*

*(The voices are slow, stifled, a prey to desire—
through this motionless body.)*

VOICE 2 (*smothered outburst*): How lovely you look
dressed in white . . .

*Pause.*

VOICE 1: I'd like to go and visit the woman of the
Ganges . . .

*Held pause.*

VOICE 1: . . . the white woman . . .
VOICE 2 (*pause*): The one who . . . ?
VOICE 1: Her . . .
VOICE 2: . . . dead in the islands . . .
VOICE 1: Eyes dead, blinded with light.
VOICE 2: Yes.
There under the stone.
In a bend in the Ganges.

*Silence.*

*Still motionless before us, the dead woman of the
      Ganges.*
*The voices are a song so quiet it does not awaken
      her death.*
*Apparently nothing changes, nothing happens. But
      suddenly, fear.*

VOICE 1 (*low, frightened*): What is it?

*No answer.*

VOICE 1 (*as before*): What time is it?
VOICE 2 (*pause*): Four o'clock.
      Black night.

*Pause.*

VOICE 1: No one can sleep?
VOICE 2: No.

*Silence.*

*Tears on the woman's face.*
*The features remain unmoving.*
*She is weeping. Without suffering.*
*A state of tears.*
*The voices speak of the heat, they speak of desire—
      as if the voices were issuing from the weeping
      body.*

VOICE 1: The heat
    Impossible
    Terrible

                                                           *Pause.*

VOICE 2: Another storm . . .
    Approaching Bengal . . .
VOICE 1 (*pause*): Coming from the islands . . .
VOICE 2 (*pause*): The estuaries.
    Inexhaustible . . .

                                                           *Silence.*

VOICE 1: What's that sound?
VOICE 2 (*pause*): Her weeping.

                                                           *Silence.*

VOICE 1: Doesn't suffer, does she . . . ?
VOICE 2: She neither.
    A leper, of the heart.

                                                           *Silence.*

VOICE 1: Can't bear it . . . ?
VOICE 2: No.
    Can't bear it.
    Can't bear India.

                                                           *Silence.*

*A man enters through the door on the left. He too
    is wearing a black wrap.*
*He halts, looks at her.*
*Then slowly goes over to her, a statue in her tears,
    under the fan, asleep.*
*He looks at her—asleep standing up. Goes right up
    to her.*
*Passes lightly over her face a hand outspread in a
    caress. Takes his hand away, looks at it: it is
    wet from the tears.*

VOICE 2 (*very low*): She's asleep.

*With infinite precaution, the man takes up the
    weeping woman and lays her down on the floor.*
*He's the man we have already seen, the man she
    danced with at the dance in S. Thala:* MICHAEL
    RICHARDSON.
*He sits down beside the outstretched body.*
*Looks at it.*
*Uncovers the body so that it is better exposed to the
    cool—imaginary—from the fan.*
*Strokes her forehead. Wipes away the tears, the
    sweat. Caresses the sleeping body.*
*Doesn't go close. Stays there watching over her
    sleep.*
*The voices slow down to the rhythm of the man's
    movements, taking up again in a sort of sung
    complaint the themes adjacent to the main story.*

VOICE 1: He loved her more than anything in the world.
VOICE 2 (*pause*): More even than that . . .

*Silence.*

VOICE 2 *spoke as if of its own love.*

VOICE 1: Where was the girl from S. Thala?

*No answer.*

VOICE 1 (*as if reading*): "From behind the indoor plants in the bar, she watches them. (*Pause.*) It was only at dawn . . . (*Stops.*) . . . when the lovers were going toward the door of the ballroom that Lola Valérie Stein uttered a cry."

*Silence.*

*In the distance, a regular cry in Hindustani. Someone selling something again.*
*It stops.*
*Quiet.*

VOICE 2: At four in the morning, sometimes, sleep comes.

*Silence.*

*The lover is still beside the sleeping body.*
*He looks at it.*

*Takes the hands, touches them. Looks at them.*
*They fall back, dead.*

*Silence.*

VOICE 1: She never got over it, the girl from S. Thala?
VOICE 2: Never.
VOICE 1: They didn't hear her cry out?
VOICE 2: No.
Couldn't hear any more.
Couldn't see.

*Pause.*

VOICE (*pause*): They abandoned her? (*Pause.*) Killed
her?
VOICE 2: Yes.

*Pause.*

VOICE 1: And with this crime behind them . . .
VOICE 2 (*scarcely heard*): Yes.

*Silence.*

VOICE 1: What did the girl from S. Thala want?
VOICE 2: To go with them
See them
The lovers of the Ganges: to see them.

*Silence.*

*That is what we are doing: seeing.*
*Slowly the man lies down beside the sleeping body.*
*His hand goes on caressing the face, the body.*
*Far away, distant sounds, oars, water. Then laugh-*
*ter, a zither, fading in the distance.*
*Then it stops.*

VOICE 2: Listen . . .
Ganges fishermen . . .
Musicians . . .

*Silence again.*
*The voices speak of the heat again. Of their desire.*

VOICE 2 (*very slow*): What darkness
What heat
Unmitigated
Deathly

*Silence.*

*A voice that is clear, implacable, terrifying:*

VOICE 2: I love you with a desire that is absolute.

*No answer.*

*Silence.*

*The hand of* MICHAEL RICHARDSON—*the lover—*
*immediately stops caressing the body, as if ar-*
*rested by what* VOICE 2 *has just said.*
*It lies there where it is on the body.*

*Silence.*

*A second man enters the room. He stands in the
    doorway for a moment, looking at the lovers.*
*MICHAEL RICHARDSON's hand starts to move again,
    caressing the uncovered body.*
*The man goes over to them.*
*Like the lover, he sits down beside her.*
*The lover's hand now moves more slowly.*
*Then it stops.*
*The newcomer does not caress the woman's body.*
*He lies down too.*
*All three lie motionless under the fan.*

*Silence.*

*Rain.*
*Another storm over Bengal.*
*The sound of rain over sleep.*
*The voices are like breaths of coolness, gentle
    murmurs.*

VOICE 1: . . . rain . . .
VOICE 2: . . . yes . . .

                                    *Pause.*

VOICE 1: . . . cool . . .

                                   *Silence.*

*The sky gets lighter, but it is still night.*
*Gradually, music: Beethoven's 14th Variation on*
  *a Theme of Diabelli. Piano, very distant.*
*The rain slackens.*
*In its place, a white light. Patches of moonlight on*
  *the garden paths. No wind.*
*The three bodies, their eyes closed, sleep.*
*The voices, interwoven, in a climax of sweetness,*
  *are about to sing the legend of* ANNE-MARIE
  STRETTER. *A slow recitative made up of scraps*
  *of memory. Out of it, every so often, a phrase*
  *emerges, intact, from oblivion.*


VOICE 1: Venice.
  She was from Venice . . .
VOICE 2: Yes. The music was in Venice.
  A hope in music . . .
VOICE 1 (*pause*): She never gave up playing?
VOICE 2: No.

*Silence.*


VOICE 1 (*very slow*): Anna Maria Guardi . . .
VOICE 2: Yes.

*Silence.*


VOICE 1: The first marriage, the first post . . . ?
VOICE 2: Savannakhet, Laos.
  She's married to a French colonial official.
  She's eighteen.

VOICE 1 (*remembering*): Ah yes . . . a river . . .
      . . . she's sitting by a river. Already . . .
      Looking at it.
VOICE 2: The Mekong.
VOICE 1 (*pause*): She's silent?
      Crying?
VOICE 2: Yes. They say: "She can't get acclimatized.
      She'll have to be sent back to Europe."

*Pause.*

VOICE 1: Couldn't bear it. Even then.
VOICE 2: Even then.

*Silence.*

VOICE 1 (*visionary*): Those walls all round her?
VOICE 2: The grounds of the chancellery.
VOICE 1 (*as before*): The sentries?
VOICE 2: Official.
VOICE 1: Even then . . .
VOICE 2: Yes.
VOICE 1: Even then, couldn't bear it.
VOICE 2: No.

*Silence.*

VOICE 2: One day a government launch calls. Monsieur
      Stretter is inspecting the posts on the Mekong.
VOICE 1 (*pause*): He takes her away from Savan-
      nakhet?

VOICE 2: Yes. Takes her with him.
Takes her with him for seventeen years through the
capitals of Asia.

*Pause.*

VOICE 2: You find her in Peking.
Then in Mandalay.
In Bangkok.
Rangoon. Sydney.
Lahore.
Seventeen years.
You find her in Calcutta.
In Calcutta:
She dies.

*Silence.*

*The tall thin man dressed in white enters the
garden.
The voices haven't seen him.
He stops. Looks through the screens on the windows
at the three sleeping forms.
Stops, looking at her, the woman.
The voices still haven't seen him.*

VOICE 1: Michael Richardson used to go to S. Thala in
the summer.
VOICE 2: Yes.
She didn't go often.
But that summer . . .

VOICE 1: He was English, Michael Richardson?
VOICE 2: Yes. (*Pause. As if reading:*) "Michael Rich-
ardson started a marine insurance company in Ben-
gal, so that he could stay in India."
VOICE 1: Near her.
VOICE 2: Yes.


> *The man goes away. We see him, from behind,
> going slowly along the path toward the deserted
> tennis courts.*


VOICE 1: The other man who's sleeping?
VOICE 2: Passing through. A friend of the Stretters'.
She belongs to whoever wants her.
Gives her to whoever will have her.
VOICE 1 (*pause, pain*): Prostitution in Calcutta.
VOICE 2: Yes.
She's a Christian without God.
Splendor.
VOICE 1 (*very low*): Love.
VOICE 2 (*scarcely heard*): Yes . . .


> *Silence.*


> *The thin man goes toward the red bicycle propped
> against the wire around the deserted tennis
> courts.*
> *The voices have seen him.*
> *They resume very softly, in fear.*

VOICE 1: He's back in the garden.
VOICE 2: Yes . . . Every night . . .
　　Looks at her . . .

*Silence.*

*The man hesitates. Then goes up to* ANNE-MARIE
　STRETTER's *bicycle.*

VOICE 1: He never spoke to her . . .
VOICE 2: No.
　　Never went near . . .

*Halt.*

VOICE 1: The male virgin of Lahore . . .
VOICE 2: Yes . . .

*The man is beside the bicycle.*
*Puts out his hands. Hesitates.*
*Then touches it.*
*Strokes it.*
*Leans forward and holds it in his arms.*
*Stays clasping* ANNE-MARIE STRETTER's *bicycle—*
　*frozen in this gesture of desire.*

*Silence.*

*Almost imperceptibly, a movement over by the*
　*sleeping bodies. It is she.*

*As he bends over the bicycle, she, by a converse movement, sits up. In the same slow rhythm she sits up and turns toward the garden.*
ANNE-MARIE STRETTER *looks at the man in white with his arms around her bicycle.*

*Silence.*

*Suddenly the man lets go of the bicycle. Remains with his arms hanging by his sides, his hands open, in an attitude of passion and despair.*
*Sound of a man sobbing (the only sound heard directly).*
*The woman still looks, sitting with her hands flat on the ground.*
*The sobs cease.*
*The man gets up.*
*He stands facing the bicycle.*
*Then slowly turns around.*
*Sees her.*
*The woman doesn't move.*

*Silence.*

*They look at each other.*
*This lasts several seconds.*

*Silence.*

*It is the man who stops looking.*
*First he turns his face away. Then his body moves.*

*He walks away.*
*She, still sitting, watches him walk away.*
*Then, after he has slowly disappeared from sight,*
*she takes up her former position, asleep under*
*the nightmare fan.*

*Silence.*

*Stillness.*
*Sobs of the* VICE-CONSUL *in the distance.*
*Silence again.*
*In the garden the light grows dim again, murky.*
*No wind in the deserted garden.*

VOICE 2 (*afraid, very low*): The sound of your heart
frightens me . . .

*Silence.*

*Another stirring in the still mass of the three sleep-*
*ing bodies:* MICHAEL RICHARDSON'S *hand*
*reaches out to the woman's body, caresses it,*
*stays there.*
MICHAEL RICHARDSON *was not asleep.*
*The light gets dimmer still.*
VOICE 2 *is full of desire and terror.*

VOICE 2: Your heart, so young, a child's . . .

*No answer.*

*Silence.*

VOICE 2: Where are you?

*No answer.*

*Silence.*

*Shouts in the distance: the* VICE-CONSUL. *Cries of despair. Heart-rending, obscene.*

VOICE 1 (*distant*): What's he shouting?
VOICE 2: The name she used to have in Venice, in the desert of Calcutta.

*Silence.*

*The cries fade in the distance.*
*Disappear.*
VOICE 2, *all in one breath, in fear, tells the story of the crime, the crime committed in Lahore:*

VOICE 2 (*low*): "He fired a gun. One night, from his balcony in Lahore, he fired on the lepers in the Shalimar gardens."

*Silence.*

VOICE 1 *is gentle—calm and gentle:*

VOICE 1: Couldn't bear it.
VOICE 2: No.
VOICE 1: India—couldn't bear India?

VOICE 2: No.
VOICE 1: What couldn't he bear about it?
VOICE 2: The idea.

*Silence.*

*It is getting darker. The bodies grow less and less
    distinguishable. Above them the fan goes on
    turning, the blades gleaming slowly.*
*You can no longer tell one body from another.*

*Silence.*

VOICE 1: A black Lancia is speeding along the road to
    Chandernagor . . .

*No answer.*

VOICE 1 (*continuing*): . . . It was there . . . there
    that she first . . .

*The voice stops.*

VOICE 2: Yes.
    Brought back by ambulance.
    They talked about an accident . . .

*Pause.*

VOICE 1: She's been thin ever since.
VOICE 2 (*scarcely heard*): Yes.

*Beethoven's 14th Variation on a Theme of Diabelli.*
*Distant.*

*Total blackout.*

*Then, beyond the garden, gleams in the sky. Either*
*day or fire—rust-colored fire.*
*The voice is slow: a calm declaration.*

VOICE 1: Those gleams over there?
VOICE 2: The burning-ghats.
VOICE 1: Burning people who've starved to death?
VOICE 2: Yes.
It will soon be daylight.

*Silence.*

*The 14th Variation is heard till the end, over the*
*gleams from the burning-ghats.*

*Blackout.*

# II

*We are in the same place as before.*

*The only difference is that the right side of it is now revealed, as if the angle of vision had been changed. Doors opening on the reception rooms on one side, and on the other on the garden.*

*(As if these rooms were in a wing of the Embassy.)*

*Bright light everywhere. Chandeliers.*

*Chinese lanterns in the garden.*

*Silence.*

*It is as if the French Embassy were quite empty.*

*Nothing can be seen of the reception rooms except the light coming out of the doors and illuminating the garden.*

*All remains empty for a few seconds.*

*Then, without a sound, a servant passes through.*

*Carrying a tray with glasses of champagne, he goes through and out toward the right.*

*Silence again. Emptiness again.*

*Waiting.*

*Then, suddenly, noise.*

*The noise of the reception begins quite suddenly, full volume. The party is triggered off as if by some mechanism: the noise bursts forth instantaneously from behind the walls, through the open doors.*

*A woman is singing "The Merry Widow," accompanied by a piano and two violins.*

*Behind the music:*

*The sound of many conversations all merging into one.*

*The sound of glasses, crockery, etc.*

*But the feet of the dancers make no sound.*

*No conversation will take place on the stage, or be seen. It will never be the actors on the stage who are speaking.*

*The only exception to this rule is that the sobs of the French* VICE-CONSUL *are both seen and heard.*

*When the conversations recorded here take place, the sound of the reception grows fainter.*

*Often it* almost *stops: for example, during the conversations between the* YOUNG ATTACHÉ *and* ANNE-MARIE STRETTER, *and between her and the French* VICE-CONSUL. *It is as if the guests at the reception, intrigued, watched them talking instead of talking themselves. So the fading of the sound is not arbitrary.*

*All the conversations, whether private or not, whether they make the guests around them go quiet or not, should give the impression that only the spectators hear them clearly—not the guests.*

*So the sound of the reception should be heard, however faintly, behind all the conversations. The fact that these conversations are now and again mingled with conversations on other subjects should prove that the private conversations are not audible, or hardly, to the guests. So also the fact that some of what is overheard is sometimes repeated, but always more or less wrongly —with slight mistakes which show that only the spectators hear the private conversations properly.*

*The sound of the reception should come from the right and from the stage, and from the auditorium, as if the reception were taking place beyond the walls of the auditorium, too.*

ANNE-MARIE STRETTER *wears a black dress—the one she wore at the dance in S. Thala—the one described in* Le Ravissement de Lol. V. Stein.

*The men wear black dinner jackets, with the exception of the French* VICE-CONSUL *in Lahore, who wears a white one.*

*The other women at the reception wear long dresses, colored.*

*The reception overflows, all the time it lasts, either into the garden or into the place we already know:* ANNE-MARIE STRETTER's *private drawing room.*

*From the point of view of sound, the image, the stage, plays the part of an echo chamber. Passing through that space, the voices should sound, to the spectator, like his own "internal rending" voice.*

*The set should seem accidental—stolen from a*

"*whole*" *that is by its nature inaccessible, that is, the reception.*

*The diction should in general be extremely precise. It should not seem completely natural. During rehearsals some slight defect should be settled on, common to all the voices.*

*One ought to get the impression of a reading, but one which is reported, that is, one which has been performed before. That is what is meant by a "reading-to-himself voice."*

*To repeat: not a single word is uttered on the stage.*

*"Heure exquise"* sung by a woman. Then repeated by the orchestra.

*A waltzing couple cross a corner of the garden.*

    *Some women are talking (quite close):*
    ——— This is the last reception before the monsoon.
    ——— What? Do you mean to say the monsoon hasn't begun?
    ——— Not really. It'll be at its height in a fortnight. No sun for six months . . . You'll see . . . No one can sleep . . . They just wait for the storms to break . . .

    *An Indian servant passes through, on his way to the reception. He carries a tray with brimming glasses of champagne.*

*Two couples go through, waltzing. Slowly. Dis-
appear.*

*Some women are talking (farther away):*
———— She invited the French Vice-consul in
Lahore . . .
———— Yes. At the last minute she sent him a
card: "Come." The Ambassador didn't say
anything.

*A young man arrives. He stops and looks around.
Clearly he isn't familiar with this part of the
Embassy. He looks tired, as if he wants to get
away from the reception. He looks out toward
the deserted tennis courts.*
*As he looks, a couple dance across a corner of the
garden and disappear.*

*Some men are talking (about the young man):*
———— Who is he?
———— The new Attaché . . . Only been out
here a month . . . He can't get used to it.
———— It's the first time he's been here.

*Pause.*

———— He'll be back. He'll be invited, he'll go
to the islands . . . The Ambassador asks
people to stay there. For her—for his wife.

*Pause.*

——— What makes you think *he'll* be asked?

*Pause.*

——— He looks so troubled . . . She doesn't
like people who get used to it.
——— Are there any?
——— Some . . .
——— Clubs, to keep India out, that's the
answer . . . isn't it?
——— Yes.

*The* YOUNG ATTACHÉ *goes on looking around. Then
he turns toward the dancing, watches the re-
ception. And goes back to it.*
*"Heure exquise" ends.*
*There is a moment without music.*
*Only the sound of the reception. No laughter. A
sort of general dejection.*
*Some women go by in the garden, looking curiously
toward* ANNE-MARIE STRETTER's *drawing room.
They fan themselves with big white fans.*
*They are gone.*

*A man speaks (the Ambassador):*
——— I think my wife may have mentioned
it . . . we'd be very glad if you'd join us
some time in the islands . . . There are
some newcomers one feels specially attracted
to . . . And the rules governing ordinary
society don't apply here . . . We don't

choose . . . (*A smile in the voice.*) You
will? The residency looks out on the Indian
Ocean, it dates from the days of the Company, it's worth seeing. And the islands are
very healthy, especially the main one, it's
the biggest island in the Delta.

*Silence.*

*Men talking:*
———— He used to write, the Ambassador . . .
Did you know? I've read a little volume of
his poems . . .
———— So I've heard . . . They say it's be-
cause of her he gave it up . . .

*"Heure exquise" has been followed by a tango.*
*The French* VICE-CONSUL *in Lahore has come into*
*the garden. He is wearing a white dinner jacket.*
*He is alone. No one seems to have noticed him*
*yet.*

*Two conversations (1 and 2) between men and*
*women:*

### No. 1
———— She might have spared us the embar-
rassment . . .

*Pause.*

———— What exactly did he do? I never know
what goes on . . .
———— The worst possible thing . . . How
can I explain . . . ?
———— The worst . . . ?

*Silence.*


## No. 2

———— An intriguing woman. No one really
knows how she spends her time . . .
What does she do? She must do something . . .
———— She must read . . . Between her
siesta and when it's time to go out, what
else could she do . . .
———— Parcels of books come for her from
Venice . . . And she spends some time
with her daughters . . . In the dry season they play tennis—you see all three
of them going by the office, dressed in
white . . .

*Pause.*


———— The fact that one wonders what she
does, that's what's strangest of all.

*Silence.*

No. 1 (*continued*)
——— Did he kill somebody?
——— He used to fire shots at the Shalimar
gardens at night . . . You knew that . . . ?
But bullets were found in the mirrors of
his own residence in Lahore . . .
——— He was shooting at himself . . .
(*Little laugh.*)

*No answer.*

——— It's difficult to tell which are the
lepers . . .
——— You see, you do know: you talk about
the lepers . . .

*Silence.*

No. 2 (*continued*)
——— She goes cycling too, very early in
the morning, in the grounds. Not during
the monsoon, of course . . .

No. 1 (*continued*)
——— What's the official version?
——— His nerves gave way . . . Often hap-
pens.

*Pause.*

——— Funny, he forces you to think about
him . . .

MICHAEL RICHARDSON *has entered. He is not wear-*
*ing a dinner jacket. He sits down. He smokes*
*a cigarette. He doesn't look toward the garden.*
*In the garden, the* VICE-CONSUL: *he looks at*
MICHAEL RICHARDSON.
*Two women enter on the right, and stop. They*
*have seen* MICHAEL RICHARDSON *and look at*
*him with curiosity. He doesn't see them.*
*A servant goes by with glasses of champagne. He*
*offers one to* MICHAEL RICHARDSON, *and goes.*
*The tango, as if in the distance.*
MICHAEL RICHARDSON *gets up, begins to go toward*
*the reception, looks at it from some distance,*
*then turns around: sees the* VICE-CONSUL *in the*
*garden.*
*Then the women see him too and draw back.*

*Women speaking (low):*
——— Look . . . Michael Richardson . . .

*Pause.*

——— Yes . . . He doesn't attend receptions?
——— No, only at the end, toward the middle
of the night. When there's just a few friends
left . . .

*Pause.*

——— What a business . . . what love . . .
They say he gave up everything to be with
her . . .

———— Everything. He was engaged to be married. Everything. Overnight . . .

*Silence.*

MICHAEL RICHARDSON *makes a movement toward the* VICE-CONSUL—*toward the gate into the garden.*
*The* VICE-CONSUL *turns away.*
MICHAEL RICHARDSON *stops.*
*The two women watch.*

*Women talking* (*low, afraid*):
———— Look in the garden . . .
———— Is that him?
———— Yes.
———— So thin . . . and the face . . . as if it were grafted on . . . so pale . . .

*Silence.*

MICHAEL RICHARDSON *turns back toward the reception.*
*The watching women disappear.*

*Women* (*continued*):
———— Do they know each other?
———— Evidently not . . .

*Silence.*

*The* VICE-CONSUL *looks at the reception.* MICHAEL RICHARDSON *looks again at him. The* VICE-CONSUL *seems absorbed, and does not notice him.*

*Men talking:*
———— He used to fire shots at night from his balcony.
———— Yes. He used to shout too. Half naked.
———— What?
———— Disconnected words. He used to laugh.

*Pause.*

———— And no woman was ever close enough to him, in Lahore, to be able to say anything . . .?
———— No. Never.
———— How is that possible?
———— His house, no one ever went to his house in Lahore . . .
———— It's terrifying . . . Such abstinence . . . Terrible . . .

*Silence.*

MICHAEL RICHARDSON *turns toward the reception, tries to make out what the* VICE-CONSUL *can be watching so avidly.*

*Men and women:*

———— Did you hear? The Ambassador said to
the Young Attaché: "People avoid him, I
know . . . he frightens them . . . But I'd
be grateful if you'd go and have a word
with him."

*Pause.*

———— What's known about his background?
his childhood?

———— His father was a bank manager in
Neuilly. An only child. The mother's supposed to have left the father. Expelled from
several schools for bad behavior. Brilliant
at his work, but after high school . . .
That's all . . .

———— So they don't know anything about him
really?

———— Nothing.

*Pause.*

———— Isn't there in all of us . . . how shall
I put it . . . ? a chance in a thousand we
might be like him . . . I mean . . .
(*Pause.*) I'm only asking . . .

*No answer.*

*Silence.*

*A couple come to the edge of the garden. They see
the* VICE-CONSUL, *and don't go any farther.*
MICHAEL RICHARDSON *looks at them. They
hesitate. Turn away. Go back to the reception.*
*The* VICE-CONSUL *looks at the reception and laughs.*
*Some women go through the garden fanning them-
selves. They don't see the* VICE-CONSUL. *They
stop and look at the reception from a distance:
something catches their attention:*

*Women:*
—————— Who's she dancing with?
—————— The Ambassador.
—————— You knew he took her away from some
official in the wilds of French Indochina
. . . I can't quite remember where . . .
Laos, I think . . .
—————— Savannakhet?
—————— That's it . . .
—————— Don't you remember? ". . . slow
launch with awnings, slow journey up the
Mekong to Savannakhet . . . wide expanse
of water between virgin forest, gray paddy-
fields . . . and in the evening, clusters of
mosquitoes clinging to the mosquito nets
. . ."
—————— What a memory! (*Little laugh.*)

*Silence.*

———— Seventeen years they've been wander-
ing around Asia.

*Silence.*

*They all look toward the reception, toward the
Ambassador dancing with his wife.*
*The* VICE-CONSUL *laughs silently.*

*Men:*
———— Has he ever talked to anyone about
Lahore?
———— Never.
———— About anything else?
———— I don't think so . . . He gets letters
from France. An elderly aunt . . . The
letters were intercepted . . . Apparently
. . . he told the Secretary of the European
Club he was in a reformatory . . . when
he was fifteen . . . in the North . . .
———— He talks to him, then? That drunk?
———— Well . . . the other one's asleep, so
really he's talking to himself . . . (*Little
laugh.*)
———— So he doesn't talk to anyone then . . .
———— That's right . . . (*Little laugh.*)
———— What did he find in India to set him
off? Didn't he know about it before? Did
he actually have to see it? It's not so difficult
to find out . . .

*Women:*

———— There are moments when he seems happy. Look . . . As if he were suddenly madly happy . . .

*Pause.*

———— Perhaps when she dances . . .
———— What an idea . . .
———— I've only just noticed . . .

*Silence.*

———— Who mentioned Bombay?
———— He did, to the Secretary at the Club. He saw himself being photographed beside the Sea of Oman on a chaise longue . . . (*Little laugh.*)
———— He doesn't talk about it any more, apparently.

*Silence.*

*The* YOUNG ATTACHÉ *has now entered the garden. He goes toward the French* VICE-CONSUL, *slowly, as if not to frighten him. The* VICE-CONSUL *makes as if to run away. The* YOUNG ATTACHÉ *hesitates, then takes him by the arm. The* VICE-CONSUL *doesn't attempt to run away any more.*

*The* YOUNG ATTACHÉ *signs to the* VICE-CONSUL *to
go with him.*
*They go toward the reception. Go in.* MICHAEL
RICHARDSON *has seen them—he is the only one
not watching* ANNE-MARIE STRETTER *dancing
with her husband.*

*Women:*
——— Did you see . . . . ?

> *Pause.*

——— Yes, it's her he's looking at  . . .

> *Pause.*

——— If you ask me, Bombay's too popular,
they'll send him somewhere else  . . .

> *Silence.*

——— Tell me about Madame Stretter.
——— Irreproachable. Outside the kitchens
you'll see big jars of cold water put out for
the beggars . . . It's she who . . .
——— . . . Irreproachable . . . (*Little laugh.*)
Come, come . . .
——— Nothing that shows. That's what we
mean here by irreproachable.

> *Silence.*

*Several people go into the garden and look toward the reception. Women fan themselves. (It is to be remembered that it's never those who are seen that speak.)*

*A man and a woman:*
—————— She looks . . . imprisoned in a kind of suffering. But . . . a very old suffering . . . too old to make her sad any more . . .

*Pause.*

—————— And yet she cries . . . People have seen her . . . in the garden . . . sometimes . . .
—————— The light perhaps, it's so harsh . . . and her eyes are so pale . . .
—————— Perhaps . . . What grace . . . Look . . .
—————— Yes . . .
—————— Frightening . . . don't you think?

*Silence.*

MICHAEL RICHARDSON *has sat down on the left side of the room. He looks as if he is waiting. He doesn't look toward the reception. He is clearly visible. Very handsome. Younger than* ANNE-MARIE STRETTER. *Obviously shy.*
*He is smoking. He is tense, absorbed.*

*Several conversations take place between people,
some of whom have and some of whom have not
seen the* VICE-CONSUL *go into the reception.*

*Women:*
——— The roses are sent direct from Nepal
. . .
——— She gives them away when the dance is
over.
——— (*Low*) Look . . . there he is . . .

*Silence.*

——— He doesn't notice everyone is looking
at him . . .
——— You can hardly see his eyes . . .
——— His face looks dead . . . Don't you
think so? . . . Frightening . . .
——— Yes. The laugh looks . . . stuck on
. . . (*Pause.*) What's he laughing at?
——— Who knows?

*Pause.*

——— In the gardens, on the way to the office,
he whistles "India Song."
——— What work does he do?
——— Filing . . . nothing much . . . just
to keep him occupied . . .

*Silence.*

*Men:*
———— It's strange—most women in India have
very white skins . . .
———— They live out of the sun. Closed shutters
. . . they're recluses . . .
———— And they don't do anything out here
. . . they're waited on.
———— Yes, they just rest.

*Silence.*

———— I admit I have a look when she and her
daughters go by on their way to play tennis
. . . In shorts . . . Women's legs seem so
beautiful here . . . walking through all
that horror . . . ( *Pause, then a start.* )
But look . . .

*Silence.*

*Women:*
———— The first thing to see is the islands . . .
———— They're so beautiful . . . I don't know
what we'd do here without them.
———— That's what we'll miss about India—
the islands in the Indian Ocean . . .

*Silence.*

*Isolated woman's voice:*
———— The best thing during the monsoon

. . . did you know? . . . hot green tea,
the way the Chinese make it . . .

*Silence.*

*Women:*
———— Do you see? The Young Attaché's talking to the Vice-consul from Lahore . . .

*Silence.*

———— The voice . . . listen to the voice . . .
how blank it is . . .

*Silence.*

*Almost total silence. Everyone looks at the* YOUNG
ATTACHÉ *and the* VICE-CONSUL.
(*The* VICE-CONSUL'*s voice is harsh, almost strident.
The* YOUNG ATTACHÉ'*s voice is low and soft.*)

*Young Attaché and Vice-consul:*
V.-CONSUL: Yes, it's difficult, of course. But
what is it with you, exactly?
Y. ATTACHÉ: The heat, naturally. But also the
monotony . . . the light . . . no color . . .
I don't know if I shall ever get used to it.
V.-CONSUL: As bad as that?
Y. ATTACHÉ: Well . . . I wasn't prejudiced
before I left France . . . What about you?

before Lahore? would you have preferred
somewhere else?

v.-CONSUL: No. Lahore was what I wanted.

*Silence.*
*Then "India Song."*

*Man and woman (low):*
———— Did you hear?
———— Not very clearly. I thought he said:
"Lahore was what I desired". . .
———— I heard: "what I . . . what I'd
. . ."
———— And what does it mean? Nothing
. . .
———— (*In one breath.*) The report said
people used to see him at night through
his bedroom window, walking up and
down as if it was broad daylight . . .
and talking . . . always to himself . . .
———— . . . At night . . . as if it was
broad daylight . . .
———— Yes . . .

*Silence.*

*One man's voice is heard dominating all the others.*

*Man (George Crawn):*
———— Come over to the bar. Allow me to
introduce myself. An old friend of Anne-

Marie Stretter's. George Crawn . . .
Serve yourselves . . . there isn't a bar-
tender . . .

*Hubbub for a few seconds—people going over to the*
*bar.*

*Woman:*
———— He said that to distract people's
attention . . .

*The noise dies down.*

    Y. ATTACHÉ: Come over to the bar. (*Pause.*)
        What are you afraid of?

*No answer.*

    Y. ATTACHÉ: They say you'd like to go to
        Bombay?
    V.-CONSUL: Won't they let me stay in Calcutta?
    Y. ATTACHÉ: No.
    V.-CONSUL: In that case I leave it to the authori-
        ties. They can send me where they like.
    Y. ATTACHÉ: Bombay's not so crowded, the
        climate's better, and it's pleasant to be by the
        sea.

*Silence.*

*Isolated man's voice:*
———— It's as if he didn't hear when you
speak to him.

    Y. ATTACHÉ: What are you doing? Come
       along . . .
    V.-CONSUL: I'm listening to "India Song."
       (*Pause.*) I came to India because of it.

                      *Silence.*


ANNE-MARIE STRETTER *appears on the stage for the
first time in Act II. She has come from the reception. She smiles at* MICHAEL RICHARDSON.
*He stands, and watches her coming. He doesn't
smile. No one sees them* (*everyone is watching
the* VICE-CONSUL *and the* YOUNG ATTACHÉ). *It
was she whom* MICHAEL RICHARDSON *was waiting for.*
ANNE-MARIE STRETTER *and* MICHAEL RICHARDSON
*look at each other.*
*He puts his arms around her.*
*They dance in a corner of the room, alone.*
*We hear the* public *voice of the* VICE-CONSUL.

    V.-CONSUL: That tune makes me want to love.
       I never have.

                   *No answer.*

                     *Silence.*

*The last speech was delivered while we could see
   the couple dancing.*
*The couple disappear, left.*
*"India Song" still.*

> V.-CONSUL: I'm sorry.
>    I didn't ask to see my file. But you know it.
>    What do they say?
> Y. ATTACHÉ: They say Lahore . . . What you
>    did in Lahore . . . People can't understand
>    it, no one can, no matter how they try . . .
> V.-CONSUL (*pause*): No one?

*No answer.*

*Silence.*

*The* BEGGAR WOMAN *appears in the garden.*
*She hides behind a bush.*
*Stays there.*

> *Men:*
> ———— He said it was impossible for him to
>    give a convincing explanation of what he
>    did in Lahore.
> ———— . . . convincing . . . ?
> ———— I was particularly struck by the word.

ANNE-MARIE STRETTER *comes back, from the left
   side of the room. Slowly. She stops. She looks*

*toward the garden: the two women of the
Ganges look at each other.*
*The* BEGGAR WOMAN, *unafraid, sticks her bald head
out, then hides again.*
ANNE-MARIE STRETTER *walks away, with the same
slow step.*

*Women:*
———— She goes to the islands alone. The Ambassador goes hunting in Nepal.
———— Alone . . . well . . .
———— With him—Michael Richardson. And
others . . .
———— They say her lovers are Englishmen,
foreigners from the embassies . . . They
say the Ambassador knows . . .
———— It's only what he expected when he met
her . . . he's older than she is . . .

*Pause.*

———— There's a friendship between them now
that's proof against anything . . .

*Silence.*

ANNE-MARIE STRETTER *has gone into the reception.*
*"India Song" ends.*
*The* VICE-CONSUL *goes back into the garden.*

*He is near the* BEGGAR WOMAN, *but they don't see
    each other.*
*A blues.*

> *Men and women:*
> —————— Protocol requires everyone to have one
> dance with the Ambassador's wife . . .
> —————— Look . . . He's left the Young Attaché
> . . . He's gone back into the garden . . .
> —————— Again . . . Ever since the beginning
> of the evening he's kept going back there . . .
> —————— As if he was on the point of running
> away.
> —————— And yet at the same time . . .

> > > > > > *Silence.*

*The* VICE-CONSUL *stands motionless, staring at the
    reception with all his might.*

> *Men and women* (*continued*):
> —————— What's he looking at?
> —————— The Ambassador's wife dancing with
> the Young Attaché.

> > > > > > *Silence.*

*The* YOUNG ATTACHÉ *and* ANNE-MARIE STRETTER
    *dance into the room, then back to the reception.
    They too create a silence around them.*

*Women* (*low*):

———— Did you hear? (*Pause.*) She said
to him: "I wish I were you, arriving in
India for the first time during the summer monsoon." (*Pause.*) They're too far
away . . . I can't hear any more . . .

> *Conversation between Anne-Marie Stretter
> (voice marvelous in its sweetness) and the
> Young Attaché:*
>
> A.-M. S. (*deliberate repetition with slight error*):
> I wish I were you, coming here for the first
> time in the rains. (*Pause.*) You're not
> bored? What do you do? In the evenings?
> On Sundays?
>
> Y. ATTACHÉ: I read . . . I sleep . . . I don't
> really know . . .
>
> A.-M. S. (*pause*): Boredom is a personal thing,
> of course. One doesn't know what to advise.
>
> Y. ATTACHÉ: I don't think I'm bored.

*Pause.*

> A.-M. S.: And then . . . (*stops*) . . . perhaps
> it's not so important as people make out
> . . . Thank you for the parcels of books,
> you send them on from the office so
> quickly . . .
>
> Y. ATTACHÉ: A pleasure . . .

*Silence.*

*The noise gradually starts up around them again,
faintly.*

Men (*in the silence of the preceding conversation*):
———— What an intriguing woman. All
those books. Those sleepless nights in
the residency in the Delta . . .
———— Yes . . . What can be behind that
sweetness . . . ?
———— Nearly every smile is enough to
break your heart . . .

                              *Silence.*

A.-M.S.: One might say practically nothing is
. . . one can do practically nothing in
India . . .
Y. ATTACHÉ (*gentle*): You mean . . . ?
A.-M. S.: Oh . . . nothing . . . the general-de-
spondency . . . (*There is a smile in her
voice.*)

Men and women:
———— They say she sometimes has had
. . . attacks . . .
———— (*Low*) You mean . . . the trip to
Chandernagor?
———— Yes. And something else . . .
sometimes she shuts herself up in her

room . . . No one can see her . . .
———— Except him, Michael Richardson
. . .
———— Yes, of course . . .

    A.-M. S.: It's neither painful nor pleasant living
in India. Neither easy nor difficult. It's nothing, really . . . nothing . . .

    Y. ATTACHÉ (*pause*): You mean it's impossible?

    A.-M. S.: Well . . . (*Charming frivolity in her
voice.*) . . . yes . . . perhaps . . . (*Smile
in her voice.*) But that's probably an over-
simplification . . .

*Men and women:*
———— She used to give concerts in Venice
. . . She was one of the hopes of Euro-
pean music.
———— Was she very young when she left
Venice?
———— Yes. She went away with a French
civil servant that she left for Stretter.

                        *Silence.*

    Y. ATTACHÉ: They say you're a Venetian.

    A.-M. S.: My father was French. My mother . . .
yes, she was from Venice.

                        *Silence.*

*Men and women (continued):*
——— She plays nearly every evening. In
the dry season, that is. (*Pause.*) During
the monsoon it's so damp pianos get out
of tune overnight . . .

> *Silence.*

Y. ATTACHÉ: The first time I saw you I thought
    you were English.
A.-M. S.: That does sometimes happen.

> *Pause.*

Y. ATTACHÉ: Are there any who never get used
    to it?
A.-M. S. (*slowly*): Nearly everyone gets used
    to it.

> *Silence.*

Y. ATTACHÉ (*suddenly crisp*): The French
    Vice-consul in Lahore is looking at you.

> *No answer.*

Y. ATTACHÉ: He's been looking at you all eve-
    ning.

> *No answer.*

Y. ATTACHÉ: Haven't you noticed?

*She avoids answering.*

A.-M. S.: Where is he hoping to be posted, do
you know?
Y. ATTACHÉ (*he knows*): Here in Calcutta.
A.-M. S.: Really . . .
Y. ATTACHÉ: I imagined you knew.

*No answer.*

*Silence.*

*Servants pass through.*
*Dances follow one another: blues, tangos, foxtrots.*

A.-M. S.: Did my husband tell you? We'd like to
invite you to the islands.
Y. ATTACHÉ: I'll be very pleased to come.

*Silence.*

*Man and woman:*
———— If you listen closely, the voice has
certain Italian inflections . . .

*Pause.*

———— Yes . . . Perhaps it's that . . .
the foreign origin . . . that makes her
seem . . . far away?

———— Perhaps . . .

A.-M. S.: You write, I believe?

Y. ATTACHÉ (*pause*): I once thought I could.
Before. (*Pause.*) Did someone tell you?

A.-M. S.: Yes, but I'd probably have guessed . . .
(*Smile in the voice.*) From your way of
being silent . . .

Y. ATTACHÉ (*smiling*): I gave it up. (*Pause.*)
Monsieur Stretter used to write too?

A.-M. S.: Yes, it did happen, to him too. And then
. . . (*She stops.*)

Y. ATTACHÉ (*pause*): And you?

A.-M. S.: I've never tried . . .

Y. ATTACHÉ (*crisply*): You think it's not worth
it, don't you . . . ?

A.-M. S. (*smile*): Well . . . (*She stops.*) Well,
yes, if you like . . .

> *Pause.*

Y. ATTACHÉ: You play.

A.-M. S.: Sometimes. (*Pause.*) Not so much, the
last few years . . .

Y. ATTACHÉ (*gently; love already*): Why?

A.-M. S. (*slowly*): It's hard to put it into
words . . .

> *Long pause.*

Y. ATTACHÉ: Tell me.

A.-M. S.: For me . . . for some time . . .

there's been a kind of pain . . . associated
with music . . .

*No answer.*

*Silence.*

*The* VICE-CONSUL *moves from where he was stand-*
*ing in the garden and goes into the reception.*
*The people still going back and forth between*
*the garden and the reception watch him.*
*A certain commotion. Some stifled exclamations.*
*Then two or three couples come into the garden, as*
*if they were running away from the man from*
*Lahore.*

*Woman:*
———— What's happening?
———— The Vice-consul from Lahore has
asked the wife of the First Secretary at
the Spanish Embassy to dance . . .

*Pause.*

———— Poor woman . . . But what are
people afraid of?
———— They're not afraid . . . It's more
a sort of . . . repulsion . . . But it's
. . . involuntary . . . you can't analyze
it . . .

*Silence.*

Y. ATTACHÉ: Will you have to dance with him?

A.-M. S.: I don't have to do anything, but . . .
(*Smile in the voice.*)

*Pause.*

Y. ATTACHÉ: Last night he was in the garden.
By the tennis courts.

*The answer comes slowly.*

A.-M. S.: I think he sleeps badly.

*Pause.*

Y. ATTACHÉ: He's still looking at you.

*Silence.*

*Isolated woman's voice:*
————— Poor woman . . . and on top of
that she feels obliged to talk to him . . .

*Silence.*

Y. ATTACHÉ: Repulsion is a feeling you know
nothing about?

*Pause.*

A.-M. S.: I don't understand . . . How could one know nothing about it?

Y. ATTACHÉ (*low*): The horror . . .

*No answer.*

*Silence.*

Y. ATTACHÉ (*very clear and distinct*): They're talking about leprosy.

*Silence.*

*The* YOUNG ATTACHÉ *was referring to the conversation between the* VICE-CONSUL *and the wife (Spanish) of the Secretary at the Spanish Embassy.*

*Vice-consul and Spanish Woman:*

SP. W. (*accent*): . . . the wife of one of our secretaries was going mad, thinking she'd caught it . . . impossible to get the idea out of her head . . . she had to be sent back to Madrid . . .

V.-CONSUL: She had leprosy?

SP. W. (*astonished*): Of course not! . . . accidents are very rare . . . in three years I only know of a ballboy at the Club . . . all the staff are examined regularly . . . most thorough . . . I

shouldn't have mentioned it . . . I don't
know how it happened . . .

V.-CONSUL: But I'm not frightened of
leprosy.

SP. W.: Just as well, because . . . Of
course, there are worse places . . .
Take Singapore . . .

V.-CONSUL (*interrupting*): Don't you understand? I want to catch it.

*Slight commotion.*

*Then silence.*

*Man and woman:*
———— She left him in the middle of the
dance . . . What happened?
———— He must have said something . . .
something that frightened her . . .

*Silence.*

*Some guests leave the garden and go back into the
reception.*
*The* BEGGAR WOMAN *sticks her bald head out and
watches—like an owl. Then hides again. The*
YOUNG ATTACHÉ *must have seen her.*

Y. ATTACHÉ: There's a beggar woman in the
garden.

A.-M. S.: I know . . . She's the one who sings

—didn't you know? Of course, you've only just arrived in Calcutta . . . I think she sings a song from Savannakhet . . . That's in Laos . . . She intrigues us . . . I tell myself I must be mistaken, it's not possible, we're thousands of miles from Indochina here . . . How could she have done it?

Y. ATTACHÉ (*pause*): I've heard her in the street, early in the morning . . . It's a cheerful song.

A.-M. S.: The children sing it in Laos . . . She must have come down through the river valleys. But how did she cross the mountains —the Cardamon Hills?

Y. ATTACHÉ: She's quite mad.

A.M. S.: Yes, but you see . . . she's alive. Sometimes she comes to the islands. How? No one knows.

Y. ATTACHÉ: Perhaps she follows you. Follows white people?

A.-M. S.: That happens. Food.

*Some guests leave the reception. Slight fear.*

*Men and women:*
——— Where is he?
——— Over by the bar . . . He drinks too much, that fellow. It'll end badly.
——— There's something . . . impossible . . . about him.
——— Yes.

———— And no one invited him anywhere in
Lahore either?

———— No.

———— He went through hell in Lahore.

———— Yes, but . . . How can one overcome
this . . . this disgust . . . ?

*Men:*

———— He's anger personified.

———— Against whom? Against what?

*No answer.*

*Silence.*

*Women:*

———— He used to call down death on Lahore,
fire and death.

———— Perhaps he drank?

———— No, no . . . Out here, drinking affects
us all in the same way—we talk about going
home . . . No, he wasn't drunk . . .

*Two women have come into the room. They are
hot, they fan themselves. They look around.*

*A blues.*

*They look at the reception.*

*Suddenly they stop fanning themselves: they've just
seen something.*

*Blues.*

*Isolated woman's voice:*
——— It was bound to happen. Look . . .
The Vice-consul from Lahore is going over
to Madame Stretter . . .

*Silence.*

*Men:*
——— Have you noticed? Out here the white
people talk about nothing but themselves
. . . The rest . . . And yet the time when
most Europeans commit suicide is during
famines . . .
——— . . . which don't cause them any suffering . . . (*Little laugh.*)

*Silence.*

*The two women watch with intense curiosity as the*
VICE-CONSUL *goes over toward Madame Stretter.*
*The sound of the reception ceases almost completely*
*for a few seconds.*
*Then it begins again, faintly. Politely stifled ex-*
*clamations.*

*Men and women (conversations 1 and 2):*

No. 1
——— Did you see? The Ambassador . . . ?
How cleverly he got his wife out of it . . .

*Silence.*

———— Where are they going?

———— Into the other drawing room . . . Of course, the Ambassador would have had to talk to him sooner or later . . . so . . .

*Silence.*

### No. 2

———— Did you see? What diplomacy . . . everyone saw.

———— Where are they going?

———— Into the other drawing room . . . (*Pause.*) A servant's bringing them some champagne . . .

*Silence.*

### No. 1

———— Why doesn't he go? Asking to be humiliated like that . . .

### No. 2

———— He said something to the Club Secretary that keeps coming back to me . . . "At home, in Neuilly, in a drawing room, there's a big black piano—closed . . . On the music rest there's the score of 'India Song.' My mother used to play it. I could hear it from my bedroom. It's been there ever since she died . . ."

———— What is it you find so striking?
———— The image.

*Silence.*

*Silence. Blues.*
MADAME STRETTER *and the* YOUNG ATTACHÉ *are walking through the gardens.*

*Ambassador and Vice-consul:*
AMB.: If I've got it right, my dear fellow, you'd prefer Bombay? But you wouldn't be given the same job there as you had in . . . (*He hesitates.*) Lahore. It's too soon yet . . . Whereas if you stay here . . . people will forget . . . India is a gulf of indifference, really . . . If you like, I'll keep you on in Calcutta . . . Would you like me to?
V.-CONSUL: Yes.

*Silence.*

*Women (low):*
———— He told her he wanted to catch leprosy.
———— Mad . . .

*Silence.*

AMB.: Funny things, careers. The more you want one the less you make one. You can't

just make a career. There are a thousand
different ways of being a French Vice-consul
. . . If you forget Lahore other people will
forget it too . . .

v.-consul (*pause*): I don't forget Lahore.

*Silence.*

*Isolated man's voice:*
———— Only one person has anything to do
with him. The Secretary at the European
Club. A drunk.

amb.: You can't get used to Calcutta? (*No
answer.*) People put that sort of thing down
to their nerves. There are remedies, you
know.

v.-consul: No.

*Silence.*

*Woman and man* (*low*):
———— And what are they talking about?
———— The reformatory in Arras. Child-
hood. And . . . (*Stops.*)
———— And . . . ?
———— Her . . . the French Ambassador's
wife . . .

*Silence.*

AMB.: At first everyone's like that. I remember
I was, myself. You either go home or you
stay. If you stay, you have to find . . . or
rather invent . . . a way of looking at
things . . . of enduring Lahore . . .

V.-CONSUL: I couldn't.

*Silence.*

*Isolated woman's voice (low):*
———— She's gone into the garden with the
Young Attaché. (*Pause.*) I told you.

*Silence.*

AMB.: Take my advice . . . weigh up the pros
and cons . . . and if you're not . . . sure
of yourself, go back to Paris . . .

V.-CONSUL: No.

*Silence.*

AMB. In that case . . . how do you see the
future?

V.-CONSUL: I see nothing.

*Silence.*

*Women (low):*
———— After every reception the leftovers

are given to the poor. Her idea. (*Lower.*)
She's coming back . . .

*Silence.*

———— Oh, I see! The garden's full of
beggars . . . crowds of them all around
the kitchens . . .
———— The sentries have been told to let
them through.

*Silence.*

ANNE-MARIE STRETTER *and the* YOUNG ATTACHÉ
*come in again (from the left). They go toward
the reception.*
*The blues is over. Another takes up the theme of
"India Song."*
*Before entering the reception* ANNE-MARIE STRETTER
*halts, as does the* YOUNG ATTACHÉ. *They wait.*
*For there, on the other side of the room, is the man
from Lahore. Distraught, he comes toward her.
Stops. Bows. Pale.*
*The* YOUNG ATTACHÉ *makes a gesture as if to stop*
ANNE-MARIE STRETTER *from accepting.*
*She hesitates, but only for a second, and then ac-
cepts the man from Lahore's invitation to dance.*
*"India Song" becomes very distant. All conversa-
tions grow faint, become intermittent murmurs.
Almost total silence.*

*At first, the* VICE-CONSUL *and* ANNE-MARIE STRET-
TER *dance in the room.*
*The* YOUNG ATTACHÉ *watches them.*
*Then they move toward the reception.*
*The* YOUNG ATTACHÉ *moves forward, still watching*
*them.*
*Other people move toward the garden. They all look*
*toward the reception.*

CONVERSATION BETWEEN A.-M. S. AND THE
VICE-CONSUL, LOW BUT VIOLENT, VERY
SLOW:

*Long silence, before the conversation begins.*

V.-CONSUL: I didn't know that you existed.

*No answer.*

V.-CONSUL: Calcutta has become a form of hope
for me.

*Silence.*

A.-M. S.: I love Michael Richardson. I'm not free
of that love.
V.-CONSUL: I know.
I love you like that, in that love.
It doesn't matter to me.

*No answer.*

v.-consul: My voice sounds odd. Can you
    hear?
    It frightens them.

a.-m. s.: Yes.

v.-consul: Whose voice is it?

*No answer.*

v.-consul: I shot at myself in Lahore, but I
    didn't die.
    Other people separate me from Lahore. I
    don't separate myself.
    Lahore is me. Do you understand too?

*Pause. Gently.*

a.-m. s.: Yes. Don't shout.

v.-consul: No.

*Silence.*

v.-consul: You are with me about Lahore. I
    know. You are in me. I'll carry you inside
    me. (*Terrible brief laugh.*) And you'll shoot
    the Shalimar lepers with me. What can
    you do about it?

*Silence.*

v.-consul: I didn't need to dance with you to
    know you. You know that.

a.-m. s.: Yes.

*Pause.*

v.-consul: There's no need for us to go any further, you and I. (*Terrible brief laugh.*) We haven't anything to say to each other. We are the same.

*Pause.*

a.-m. s.: I believe you.

*Pause.*

v.-consul: Love affairs you have with others. We don't need that.

*Silence.*

*The* vice-consul's *voice is broken by a sob. It is no longer under his control.*

v.-consul: I wanted to know the smell of your hair—that's why I . . . (*He stops. A sob.*)

*Silence.*

*His voice returns to normal—almost.*

v.-consul: After the reception your friends stay on.
I'd like to stay with you for once.
a.-m. s.: You haven't a chance.

*Pause.*

v.-consul: They'd throw me out.
a.-m. s.: Yes.
   You're someone they have to forget.

*Pause.*

v.-consul: Like Lahore.
a.-m. s.: Yes.

*Silence.*

v.-consul: What will become of me?
a.-m. s.: You'll be posted somewhere a long way
   from Calcutta.

*Pause.*

v.-consul: That's what you want.
a.-m. s.: Yes.

*Pause.*

v.-consul: Very well. And when will it end?
a.-m. s.: When you die, I believe.

*Silence.*

v.-consul (*heart-rending*): What's this pain?
   Mine?

*Pause.*

A.-M. S.: Knowledge.

V.-CONSUL (*terrible laugh*): Of you?

*No answer.*

*Silence.*

V.-CONSUL: I'm going to shout. I'm going to ask them to let me stay tonight.

*Pause.*

A.-M. S.: (*pause*): Do as you like.

V.-CONSUL: So that something should happen between us. In public. Shouting is all I know. Let them at least find out a love can be shouted.

*No answer.*

V.-CONSUL: They'll feel uncomfortable for half an hour. Then they'll start talking again.

*No answer.*

V.-CONSUL: I even know you won't tell anyone you agreed.

*No answer.*

*Silence.*

*"India Song" ends.*
*It is replaced by "Heure exquise," sung.*
*The sky grows pale.*
*Two men, drunk, stagger in and collapse into arm-*
*   chairs.*
*Over "Heure exquise," mingled with it, the* VICE-
*   CONSUL's first cry.*

v.-consul: Let me stay!

*Silence.*

*Guests shrink back toward the garden. The two*
*drunk men laugh. The others are horrified.*

v.-consul: I'm going to stay here tonight, with
   her, for once, with her! Do you hear?

*Silence.*

*Isolated woman's voice:*
——— How awful . . .

*Isolated voice of Young Attaché:*
——— You really ought to go home, you've
   had too much to drink . . . come along . . .

*"Heure exquise" still.*
*The* VICE-CONSUL *shrieks.*

v.-consul: I'm going to stay! In the French
   Embassy!

I'm going to the islands with her!
Please! Please! Let me stay!

*Silence.*

*Isolated woman's voice* (*anguished*):
———— She looks as if she didn't hear . . .

*Another* (*the same*):
———— This is terrible . . .

*Silence.*

V.-CONSUL (*shrieking*): Once! Just once! I've never loved anyone but her!

*Silence.*

*Isolated man's voice, to Vice-consul:*
———— We're sorry, but you're the sort of person who only interests us when you're not there.

*Silence.*

*Isolated woman's voice:*
———— How cruel . . . It's terrible . . . horrible . . .                    ——

The VICE-CONSUL's *sobs. Unrestrained. All dignity swept away.*
*Everyone suddenly turns aside.*

*Isolated woman's voice:*
——— I can't bear to see it . . .

*The* VICE-CONSUL *appears, shaken with sobs. We
see and* hear *them.*
*A man, a stranger, leads him by the arm toward
the entrance of the Embassy. The* VICE-CONSUL
*resists at first, then lets himself be led away.*
*They disappear.*
*Everyone stands looking after them.*

*Isolated woman's voice:*
——— He's gone. (*Long pause.*) They're
shutting the gate.

*In the distance, the same cries: the* VICE-CONSUL *has
started to shout again.*

*Isolated woman's voice:*
——— He was laughing and crying at the
same time. Did you see?

*Silence.*

*"Heure exquise" continues imperturbably to the
end, while everyone stands looking away from
the reception and toward the* VICE-CONSUL.
*The cries still go on.*

*Isolated man's voice:*
——— He's trying to break down the gate.

*Silence.*

*"Heure exquise" ends.*
*The cries get farther away.*

> *Isolated voice:*
> ———— The beggars are frightened . . .

> *Isolated voice, the last:*
> ———— He's gone.

*Silence. A few seconds of it, then:*

*Blackout.*

*Darkness gradually blots out the picture as, in the
    far distance, the silhouette of the* BEGGAR
    WOMAN *passes by, then disappears.*

*Silence.*

*Then suddenly, on the piano, Beethoven's 14th
    Variation on a Theme of Diabelli.*

*Blackout.*

# III

# Notes on Voices 3 and 4

VOICES 3 and 4 are men's voices. The only thing that connects them is the fascination exerted on them by the story of the lovers of the Ganges, especially, once again, by that of ANNE-MARIE STRETTER.

VOICE 3 can remember almost nothing of the chronology of the story. It questions VOICE 4, and VOICE 4 answers.

Of all the voices, VOICE 4 is the one which has forgotten the story the least. It knows almost all of it.

But VOICE 3, although it has forgotten almost everything, recognizes things as VOICE 4 relates them. VOICE 4 doesn't tell it anything it didn't know before, at a time when it too knew the story very well.

The difference between VOICES 3 and 4, between forgetfulness on the one hand and remembrance on the other, arises from the same cause—the fascination the story exerts on the two voices. VOICE 3 has rejected the fascination, VOICE 4 has tolerated it.

The story of the lovers of the Ganges is *in* both voices—latent in the one, manifest in the other. About to survive or revive.

The difference—between the tolerable and the intolerable—should be reflected in the sensibilities of the two voices.

It is not without apprehension that VOICE 4 informs VOICE 3. VOICE 4 often hesitates. For VOICE 3 is exposed to the danger, not of madness, like VOICE 1, but of suffering.

*We are in the same part of the Embassy as before. There are five people there in the darkness, which slowly disappears:*

ANNE-MARIE STRETTER, MICHAEL RICHARDSON, *the* YOUNG ATTACHÉ, *the* GUEST (*friend of the Stretters*), *and an old friend, an Englishman,* GEORGE CRAWN.

*The drunk journalists have gone. The rest are by themselves, in an intimacy in which each of them feels alone. It is late, they are separated by fatigue.*

*They are waiting. Their chairs—except for those of* ANNE-MARIE STRETTER *and* MICHAEL RICHARDSON— *are too far apart for conversation.*

*The* YOUNG ATTACHÉ *and the Stretters'* GUEST *look exhausted, also, by the events of the evening.*

*We don't know what they are waiting for: perhaps*

*for it to be light, so that they can leave for the islands.
Probably.*

*We still hear Beethoven's 14th Variation on a
Theme by Diabelli. Through the music, the sounds of
Calcutta grow stronger with the light.*

ANNE-MARIE STRETTER *sits with her head flung
back and to one side over the arm of a chair. She might
seem to be asleep if it weren't for the fact that her eyes
are open.*

MICHAEL RICHARDSON *is near her, half lying on a
low chair.*

*The* YOUNG ATTACHÉ *is sitting up straight, smoking. He looks as if he is listening to the noises of Calcutta, through which one suddenly recognizes the cries,
the last spasms of the calls to love of the* VICE-CONSUL
*from Lahore. The* YOUNG ATTACHÉ *obviously finds
them hard to bear. The others do not.*

*The Stretters'* GUEST, *standing, looks around at the
others: these people of India whom he thought he knew,
but whom he scarcely recognizes after the night of the
reception. He too listens to the cries of the* VICE-CONSUL.

GEORGE CRAWN *listens to the Beethoven: he is en-
tirely absorbed by the music.*


VOICE 4: As usual after a reception, some people stayed
   on.
VOICE 3 (*low*): Is he the one sitting near her—Michael
   Richardson?
VOICE 4: Yes.

VOICE 3 (*hesitating*): Did they ever find out . . . ?
VOICE 4 (*hesitating*): After she died he left India.

*Silence.*

VOICE 4 (*continuing*): The one standing up is the
Young Attaché.
VOICE 3: And the elderly Englishman?
VOICE 4: George Crawn. He knew her in Peking.

*Pause.*

VOICE 3: And the one looking at them?
VOICE 4: Someone passing through. Stretter's guest.

*Silence.*

VOICE 3: Is that the French Vice-consul shouting?
VOICE 4: Yes. Still.

*Silence.*

VOICE 4: All trace of him disappears in 1938. (*Pause.*)
He resigns from the consular service. The resigna-
tion is the last thing on the file.
VOICE 3 (*hesitating*): Very soon afterwards . . .
VOICE 4: A few days.

*Silence. Cries.*

VOICE 3: What's he shouting?
VOICE 4: Her name.

*Pause.*

VOICE 3 (*slowly*): Anna Maria Guardi.
VOICE 4: Yes. All night, all through Calcutta, he's been
shouting that name.

*Silence.*

*The women's voices (from Act I) now arrive. They
too speak of the* VICE-CONSUL.

VOICE 2 (*as if exhausted*): He walks along by the
Ganges.
He comes on the lepers asleep.
Someone else is shouting on the other bank.

*Pause.*

VOICE 1: Yes.

*Silence.*

VOICE 2: Can you see him?
VOICE 1 (*distant*): Yes. I'm watching.
I see.

*Silence.*

VOICE 2 (*slow*): Is he looking for something? . . .
Or walking at random? . . . Aimlessly?

*No answer.*

VOICE 2: Is he looking for something he's lost?

*No answer.*

VOICE 2: Something in common that he's lost too?

*No answer.*

VOICE 2: The love of her?
VOICE 1: Love. Yes.

*Silence.*

VOICE 2 (*yearning*, *desire*): How far away you are
. . . from me . . .

*No answer.*

*Silence.*

*A  servant  goes  through  with  trays  piled  with
glasses, ashtrays, etc. He passes them as though
he didn't see them.*
*Gleams in the sky. The burning-ghats.*

VOICE 1 (*slow*): It will soon be day.

*Silence.*

VOICE 1 (*very slow*): Dawn is breaking here, all
     around.
     And there.
     The air smells of mud. And leprosy. And burning.
VOICE 2: Not a breath.
VOICE 1: No. Slow stirrings, slow movements, smells.

*Silence.*

VOICE 2: Can't I hear music?
VOICE 1: No.
VOICE 2: That sound of wings, of birds.
VOICE 1: The fan. Forgotten.

*Silence.*

*The men's voices mingle with the women's.*

VOICE 3: Those gleams.
VOICE 4: Day.
     The first zone is the zone of leprosy and dogs. They
     are on the banks of the Ganges, under the trees. No
     strength left. No pain.
VOICE 3: And those who have died of hunger?
VOICE 4: Farther away, in the density of the North.
     The last zone.

*Pause.*

VOICE 4: Day. The sun.

*Pause.*

VOICE 3: The light. Terrible.

*Silence.*

VOICE 1: The light. Of exile.
VOICE 2: Is she asleep?
VOICE 1: Which one?
VOICE 2: The white woman.
VOICE 1: No. Resting.

*Silence.*

VOICE 2 (*mournfully*): How far away you are. Quite absent.

*No answer.*

*Silence.*

MICHAEL RICHARDSON *slowly turns his head toward* ANNE-MARIE STRETTER. *Looks at her.*

VOICE 3 (*startled*): Voices near us suddenly? Did you hear?
VOICE 4 (*pause*): No . . .
VOICE 3: Young voices . . . women's?

VOICE 4 (*pause*): I don't hear anything. (*Pause.*)
Silence.

*Silence.*

VOICE 4: He's looking at her.
VOICE 3: Yes.
She is far away. Quite absent.

*Silence.*

VOICE 4 (*in one breath*): People said one day they'd
both be found dead in a brothel in Calcutta they
used to go to sometimes during the monsoon.

*Silence.*

VOICE 3: Not a breath. The heat is the color of rust.
Above, the smoke.
VOICE 4: The factories. The middle zone.

*Silence.*

*Very slowly* ANNE-MARIE STRETTER *has inclined
her head toward* MICHAEL RICHARDSON. *They
look at each other.*

VOICE 3: That overhanging mass . . . ?
VOICE 4: The monsoon.
Below, Bengal.

VOICE 3: And farther away . . . lower . . . under the clouds . . . ? Look . . .

*No answer.*

VOICE 3: That white patch . . . in a bend in the Ganges . . . ? There . . . ?
VOICE 4 (*hesitating*): The English cemetery.

*Silence.*

*The stranger and the* YOUNG ATTACHÉ *begin to look at* ANNE-MARIE STRETTER.

VOICE 1: Is she a leper?
VOICE 2: Which one?
VOICE 1: The beggar.
VOICE 2: She sleeps in leprosy, and every morning . . . No. (*Pause.*) No.

*Silence.*

VOICE 1: And the white woman?
VOICE 2: A false alarm ten years ago. But no, she neither. (*Pause.*) Listen . . .

*Sound of a machine and of water.*

VOICE 1: The water sprinklers in the English quarter.

*Silence.*

*The men turn their eyes away from* ANNE-MARIE
STRETTER *and look at the ground.*
*The stage gradually gets lighter.*

VOICE 1: A car is speeding along the straight roads.
Beside the Ganges.
VOICE 2: Black?
VOICE 1: Yes.
VOICE 2: They've left for the islands.

*Silence.*

*The fires of the ghats are out. It is daylight. Pale*
*daylight.*
*They lie there, in the same deathly attitude, as the*
*voices describe the journey.*

VOICE 4: The French Embassy's black Lancia has
started out for the Delta.

*Long silence.*

VOICE 3 (*as if reciting a lesson*): The granary of north-
ern India . . . The frontier of the waters. The
Delta.
VOICE 4: Yes, the mingling of the waters. The sweet
and the salt.
VOICE 3: After the deluge, before the light . . .

*Pause.*

VOICE 3: And those junks?
VOICE 4: Rice.
　　Sailing down to Coromandel.

*Pause.*

VOICE 3: Those dark patches on the banks?
VOICE 4: People.
　　The highest density in the world.

*Silence.*

VOICE 3: Those thousands of dark mirrors?
VOICE 4: The paddy fields of India.

*Silence.*

VOICE 4: They're asleep.
　　She's lying close to him.

*Silence.*

VOICE 3: She used to wake up late during the monsoon?
VOICE 4: Yes. Didn't go out till after dark.

*Silence.*

VOICE 3: The black Lancia has stopped.
VOICE 4: The rain. The roads are blocked.
　　They took shelter in a rest house. (*As if reading.*)
　　It was there the Young Attaché said: "I saw the
　　Vice-consul again before I left. He was still shouting

in the streets. He asked me if I was going to the
islands. I said no, I was going to Nepal with the
Ambassador."

*Pause.*

VOICE 3: Did she approve of the Young Attaché's lie?
VOICE 4: She practically never mentioned the man from
Lahore.

*Silence.*

VOICE 3: That patch of green? it's getting bigger . . .
VOICE 4: The sea.

*Silence.*

*Blackout.*

*The voices speak in the dark.*

VOICE 4: The islands.
VOICE 3: Which one?
VOICE 4: The biggest, the middle one. They're there.

*Silence.*

VOICE 3: That big white building . . . ?
VOICE 4: A big international hotel. The "Prince of
Wales."
The sea is rough. There's been a storm.

*Blackout ends.*

# IV

The same as before, but it has become a lounge in the "Prince of Wales."

They are not there.

A bright, greenish light instead of that of the monsoon.

The servants in white gloves are putting up green canvas blinds over the screened windows.

We do not recognize the garden. It has exploded into a violent green light—the garden of the "Prince of Wales." All that remains of the garden in Calcutta are some clumps of foliage.

The sound of the sea gradually spreads, increasing every second, until it invades everything. Then it remains stable.

The wind makes the blinds flap.

Sound of launches' sirens in the distance.

*Close, the cheeping of birds.*

*The fan is still there, going around at the same nightmare speed.*

*In the distance, a dance: an orchestra is playing "India Song."*

*The sounds occur one after the other. For example:*

*1. The wind.*

*2. The sea.*

*3. Sirens.*

*4. Birds.*

*5. Dance.*

*As the two servants put up the blinds, thus creating the set for the "Prince of Wales,"* VOICES *3 and 4 speak to each other.*

VOICE 4 *remains the same throughout.*

VOICE 3 *changes as the end of the story approaches. It becomes either more pressing or, conversely, less eager to question. When it speaks of* ANNE-MARIE STRETTER *it gets lower, with silences between words and phrases.*

VOICE 4: In front, the landing stages. The boats go to and from the South Pacific.
Behind, there's a yachting harbor.

*Silence.*

VOICE 3: Beyond the palms, the same flat horizon.
VOICE 4: They're alluvial islands, formed by the Ganges mud.

*Silence.*

VOICE 3: Where's the French residency?
VOICE 4: The other side of the hotel, looking out to sea.

> *The servants go out. They have "finished" the set*
> *for the "Prince of Wales." When they have*
> *gone the sound of the dance is heard in the*
> *distance.*
> *They are playing "India Song."*

VOICE 4: At this time of the day, people used to start
to drink at all the tables in the "Prince of Wales."
On the sideboards there are French grapes. In the
showcases, perfumes.
Roses are sent every day from Nepal.
VOICE 3: Who lives in this hotel?
VOICE 4: White India.

*Silence.*

VOICE 3 (*almost shouting*): What's that sudden smell
of death?
VOICE 4: Incense.

> *The smell of incense should pervade the auditorium.*

*Silence.*

VOICE 3: She wanted to go for a swim when they got
here?

VOICE 4: Yes. It was late, the sea was rough, it was impossible to swim. Just let the warm waves break over you. She and he both went in.

Silence.

VOICE 3 (*afraid*): All those screens in the sea?
VOICE 4: Protection against the sharks.
VOICE 3: Oh.

Silence.

VOICE 3: Where is she?
VOICE 4: She'll come.

Silence.

VOICE 4: Here she is.
VOICE 3 (*hesitating; lower, more slowly*): Was she like that that night . . . ?
VOICE 4 (*pause*): Smiling.
Dressed in white.

Silence.

*These last two phrases should be felt as terrifying:*
    ANNE-MARIE STRETTER's *smile, the whiteness of*
    *her dress.*
*In the green light,* ANNE-MARIE STRETTER *enters.*
*Smiling, dressed in white.*
*She goes and looks at the sea, beyond the garden.*

*The four men enter, also dressed in white, from
different parts of the hotel.*
*They all go toward the garden and look out at the
sea.*
MICHAEL RICHARDSON *turns and gazes at* ANNE-
MARIE STRETTER.
*She doesn't look at him any more.*
*In the distance, a voice over a loudspeaker.*

LOUDSPEAKER: The last boat tonight leaves at seven
o'clock.
VOICE 4: That's for the tourists who want to get back.
There's a storm threatening.

*Ships' sirens. Then silence.*

VOICE 4: The last launch has just arrived. The one that
brings supplies.

*Silence.*

*A head waiter comes and bows to the five people.
Their table is ready. They go off toward the left.
Still the distant airport music.*

VOICE 4 (*pause*): Their table's ready. The food here
is excellent.
Michael Richardson used to say that once you knew
the "Prince of Wales" you were never really satisfied
anywhere else in the world.

VOICE 3 (*low*): I can't quite remember . . . isn't she going to the French residency?

VOICE 4: She only used to sleep there.
She used to dine at the "Prince of Wales" when she stayed on the islands. (*Hesitates.*)
She'd had the servants at the residency sent back to Calcutta.

*Pause.*

*Fear.*

VOICE 3 (*low*): How long ago?

VOICE 4: A few weeks.

*Bird cries, so loud they are almost unbearable.*

VOICE 3: The birds . . . thousands of them.

VOICE 4: Prisoners on the islands. They couldn't fly back to the coast because of the storm.

VOICE 3: It's as if they were right inside the hotel . . .

VOICE 4: They're in the mango trees. They strip them. They'll fly away when it's light.

*Noise of birds swamps everything else.*

*Silence.*

VOICE 3: There's dancing at the other end of the lounge.

VOICE 4: Tourists from Ceylon.

*Silence.*

VOICE 4: During dinner . . . she asked them to raise
   the blind. She wants to see the sea, the sky, above
   the estuaries. They scarcely speak, they're very
   tired from last night.

*Silence.*

VOICE 3: She's not eating anything.
VOICE 4: Hardly anything. She's looking out of the
   window.
VOICE 3: I remember . . . A wall of mist is sweeping
   toward the islands . . .
VOICE 4: Yes. She's saying something about Venice.
   (*Effort of memory.*) Venice in the winter . . .
   yes, that's right . . .

*Pause.*

VOICE 3: Venice . . .
VOICE 4: Yes. Perhaps, some winter evenings in Venice,
   the same kind of mist . . .
VOICE 3: . . . she's saying the name of . . . (*stops*)
   of a color . . .
VOICE 4: Purple. The color of the mist in the Delta . . .

*Silence.*

*Beyond the green windows of the hotel, disheveled,
   exhausted, his features contorted, still wearing*

*his white dinner jacket, appears the French*
VICE-CONSUL. *He goes through the garden of
the hotel, searching.*
*Disappears.*
*Then reappears almost at once on the stage, now
the lounge of the "Prince of Wales," walks
across the room, looks toward the left, stops
short.*
*He has seen her.*
*He stands there looking at her.*

VOICE 3: He came over by the last boat.
VOICE 4: Yes. The seven-o'clock.

*Pause.*

He hadn't been home all day. (*Pause.*) He never
went back to Calcutta.

*Silence.*

*The tune of "India Song" is played loudly for a few
seconds, then fades.*

VOICE 3: "India Song" . . .
VOICE 4: Yes.

*Silence.*

VOICE 4: Now that the mist has come the wind has
dropped.

*Silence.*

*Some tourists go by in the garden beyond the green
windows. One can make out women fanning
themselves with white fans. Light-colored
dresses.*

VOICE 4: They're talking about the beggar woman.

*No answer.*

*Silence.*

VOICE 4: George Crawn and the Stretters' guest are
talking about the beggar woman.

*Silence.*

*FIRST VERSION: The conversation between*
GEORGE CRAWN *and the Stretters'* GUEST *is heard
as from some distance. (Very light and ordinary.)*

G. CRAWN: She doesn't know a word of Hindustani.
GUEST: Not a word. If she's from Savannakhet she
must have come through Laos, Cambodia, Siam,
and Burma, and then probably down through the
Irrawaddy Valley . . . Mandalay . . . Prome
. . . Bassein . . .
G. CRAWN: It must have been not just one journey, as
we might think, but hundreds, thousands, every

day, each one the last . . . Hunger always driving
her on, farther and farther . . . She must have
followed roads, railways, boats . . . but what's
strange is that she always went toward the sun-
set . . .

GUEST: . . . I suppose she traveled at night, and faced
toward the light . . . She's bald . . . Because of
hunger, do you think?

G. CRAWN: Yes.

*Pause.*

G. CRAWN: Sometimes she comes to the islands. Following the whites, probably: food . . . In Calcutta she
lives by the Ganges, under the trees. She gets up
at night and goes through the English quarter.
Apparently she hunts for food at night along the
Ganges.

*Pause.*

GUEST: And what's left of her in Calcutta? Not much
. . . The song of Savannakhet, the laugh . . .
and her native language is still there of course, but
there's no use for it. The madness was there when
she arrived . . . already too far gone . . .

*Pause.*

G. CRAWN: Why Calcutta? Why did her journey stop
there?

GUEST: Perhaps because she can lose herself there. She's always been trying to lose herself, really, ever since her life began . . .

*Pause.*

G. CRAWN: She too.
GUEST: Yes . . .

*Silence.*

*SECOND VERSION:* (VOICES 3 *and* 4 *relate the conversation between* GEORGE CRAWN *and the* STRETTERS' GUEST. (VOICE 4 *is the one that hears it.*)

VOICE 4: They've seen her.
She must have crossed the Delta on the roof of a bus. She stowed away on the last boat.
They met her by the lagoon, a few hundred yards from the French residency.

*Pause.*

VOICE 3: She must have been following Anne-Marie Stretter . . .
VOICE 4: The guest says she followed him to the gate. She frightened him.
He said: "That eternal smile is frightening . . ."
VOICE 3: That too . . .

VOICE 4: Yes. (*Pause.*) You remember?
The first attempt . . . (*stops*) at Savannakhet,
because of a dead child . . .
VOICE 3: . . . sold by its mother, a beggar from the
North . . . very young . . . ?
VOICE 4: Yes. Seventeen . . . (*Pause.*) A few days
before Stretter arrived.

*Silence.*

*Suddenly the* VICE-CONSUL *goes toward the right,
and disappears: he has seen them.*
*Here they are, coming out from dinner. There are
now only three of them:* ANNE-MARIE STRETTER,
MICHAEL RICHARDSON, *the* YOUNG ATTACHÉ.
*They walk across the lounge, making for the garden
through the middle door.*
*In the garden they separate.*
ANNE-MARIE STRETTER *goes to the right.*
*The others go straight on through the garden and
disappear.*
*The* VICE-CONSUL *begins to go after* ANNE-MARIE
STRETTER.
*He halts.*
*She has stopped too.*
*She looks around her at the sea, the palms.*
*She hasn't seen the* VICE-CONSUL.

VOICE 4: She wanted to walk back on her own.

*Silence.*

VOICE 4: The other two went for a sail . . .

*Silence.*

VOICE 4: The Young Attaché and Michael Richardson went back to the French residency the other way, along the beach.

*Pause.*

VOICE 4: It was as hot again as it had been in Calcutta.

ANNE-MARIE STRETTER *walks slowly away.*
*Behind her, the* VICE-CONSUL. *He is following her.*
*They disappear.*

*Blackout.*

*During the blackout, the 14th Beethoven-Diabelli*
*Variation in the distance.*

*Blackout fades.*

V

*The same as before, but it is now the French residency.*

*The light is different. It seems to come from outside. It is blue, like moonlight.*

*The fan is still there. Still going around.*

*The garden of the Embassy and the garden of the hotel have both gone. There is just an empty space. A path, and at the end of it a white gate.*

*Everything is enveloped in endless, fathomless emptiness. But it has a sound: the sea.*

*After a while,* MICHAEL RICHARDSON *and the* YOUNG ATTACHÉ *come in through the white gate.*

*Simultaneously, she enters, from the left of the house.*

*She is barefoot. Her hair is loose. She wears the short black cotton wrap.*

*She joins them on the path, they go toward one
another, meet in the half-light.
They look at the sea.*

VOICE 4: She's supposed to have said she was worried
about George Crawn and the Guest. The sea was
rough.

*Sound of a rowing boat in the distance. They all
look toward something out at sea.*

VOICE 4: She didn't have to worry any more. George
Crawn and the Guest went straight back to the
hotel without calling in at the residency.

*Silence.*

*They slowly walk back into the house.*

VOICE 3 (*pause; stricken*): She didn't say anything that
evening that might have made anyone think . . .
(*Stops.*)
VOICE 4: No. Nothing.

*Terrific tension. But nothing breaks the quiet spell
of death.*
MICHAEL RICHARDSON *goes over to the piano.*
*She goes out of the room.*
*The two men are left there alone. They look at each
other.*

*Outside, in the distance, at the end of the path, the
white shape of the* VICE-CONSUL *comes through
the open gate.*
*They don't see him.*
*She comes back, bringing glasses and champagne.
She smiles at them.*
*She puts the bottle and glasses down on a low table
and pours out the champagne.*
*She takes it to them.*
*They drink.*
*She sits down on a sofa.*
*There is still the fixed smile on* ANNE-MARIE STRET-
TER'S *face.*
*Outside, the* VICE-CONSUL *watches.*
MICHAEL RICHARDSON *plays.*

*He plays the 14th Beethoven-Diabelli Variation.*
*Complete stillness.*

*Suddenly the stillness is shattered:*
*The* YOUNG ATTACHÉ *goes over to* ANNE-MARIE
STRETTER, *puts his arms around her, then falls
at her feet, and stays there with his arms around
her legs.*
*He stays there, riveted to her.*
*She doesn't prevent him.*
*Strokes his hair.*
*Still the smile. The fixed smile.*
*He gets up. Draws her to her feet, flings his arms*

*around her body, naked under the wrap. A
gesture of supplication. Vain.*

*They kiss. A long kiss.*

MICHAEL RICHARDSON *watches. Plays the piano and
watches them. His face is as we have always
known it.*

*The white shape from Lahore gazes in avidly from
outside.*

*The* YOUNG ATTACHÉ *roughly releases* ANNE-MARIE
STRETTER, *staggers over to the piano and leans
on it with his head in his hands. The Beethoven
continues:* MICHAEL RICHARDSON *goes on playing. Stillness. Stillness enveloped in music.*

*The* YOUNG ATTACHÉ *remains leaning on the piano,
motionless. The attitude of despair itself.*

*For the last time, one of the women's voices:*

VOICE 2 (*terrified*): Where are you? (*Waits. No
answer.*)
You're so far away . . . I'm frightened . . .

> VOICE 1 *doesn't answer any more.*

> *Silence.*

ANNE-MARIE STRETTER *turns toward outside,
toward the sea.*

*Shows no surprise when she sees the* VICE-CONSUL.

*He doesn't move, makes no attempt to conceal him-
self. Gazes fixedly at her.*

*She turns and bares her body to the fan.*

*Perhaps her naked body is visible to everyone.*
*To the* VICE-CONSUL *also—the body already sep-*
*arate from her.*
*She stands there motionless under the fan.*

*Silence.*

VOICE 3 (*low, almost a murmur*): Michael Richardson
left her alone that evening?
VOICE 4 (*hesitating*): It had been agreed between the
lovers of the Ganges that they'd leave each other
free if ever either of them decided . . . (*Stops.*)

*Silence.*

VOICE 3 (*suffering, terror*): But he doesn't know, it
isn't possible . . .

*No answer.*

VOICE 3: What does he know?
VOICE 4 (*pause*): Ever since the servants were sent
away, Michael Richardson had been living with
this possibility.

*Silence.*

ANNE-MARIE STRETTER *has lain down under the*
*fan.*
*She has closed her eyes.*
MICHAEL RICHARDSON *and the* YOUNG ATTACHÉ

*slowly tear themselves away, as if she had*
*actually ordered them to leave her alone there.*
*They cross the empty space outside. Shadows.*
*The* VICE-CONSUL *is there. He doesn't hide as they*
*go past.*
*It is as if they do not see him.*
*They disappear from sight.*
ANNE-MARIE STRETTER *and the* VICE-CONSUL *from*
*Lahore are the only ones left in the French*
*residency.*

*Silence.*

*She gets up, goes out, slowly walks through the*
*empty space toward the white gate.*
*It is as if she doesn't see anything. She doesn't see*
*the* VICE-CONSUL.
*And he makes not the slightest gesture toward her.*

VOICE 3 (*scarcely breathed*): Is he the only one who
saw . . . ?
VOICE 4: He didn't say.
VOICE 3 (*as before*): . . . he didn't do anything to
stop . . .

*No answer.*

VOICE 4: The Young Attaché came back to the resi-
dency in the course of the night. He saw her.
She was lying on the path, resting on her elbow.
He said: "She laid her arm out straight and leaned

her head on it. The Vice-consul from Lahore was
sitting ten yards away. They didn't speak to each
other."

*Silence.*

*What has just been related is what* ANNE-MARIE
STRETTER *does. She lays her face on her arm.*
*Stays like that. The* VICE-CONSUL *looks at her,*
*riveted to the distance between them.*

VOICE 4: She must have stayed there a long while, till
daylight—and then she must have gone along the
path . . . (*Stops.*) They found the wrap on the
beach.

*Silence.*

*The fan stops.*
*Rest a few seconds on the stopping of the fan.*

*Blackout.*

# Summary

This summary is the only one which should accompany productions of *India Song*.

This is the story of a love affair which takes place in India in the thirties, in an overpopulated city on the banks of the Ganges. Two days in this love story are presented. It is the season of the summer monsoon.

Four voices—faceless—speak of the story. Two of the voices are those of young women, two are men's.

The voices do not address the spectator or reader. They are totally independent. They speak among themselves, and do not know they are being heard.

The voices have known or read of this love story long ago. Some of them remember it better than others. But none of them remembers it completely. And none of them has completely forgotten it.

We never know who the voices are. But just by the way each of them has forgotten or remembers, we get to know them more deeply than through their identity.

The story is a love story immobilized in the culmination of passion. Around it is another story, a story of horror—famine and leprosy mingled in the pestilential humidity of the monsoon—which is also immobilized, in a daily paroxysm.

The woman, Anne-Marie Stretter, wife of a French Ambassador to India and now dead—her grave is in the English cemetery in Calcutta—might be said to be born of this horror. She stands in the midst of it with a grace which engulfs everything, in unfailing silence—a grace which the voices try to see again, a grace which is porous and dangerous, dangerous also for some of them.

Besides the woman, in the same city, there is a man, the French Vice-consul in Lahore, in Calcutta in disgrace. It is by anger and murder that he is connected to the horror of India.

There is a reception at the French Embassy, in the course of which the outcast Vice-consul cries out his love to Anne-Marie Stretter, as white India looks on.

After the reception she drives along the straight roads of the Delta to the islands in the estuary.

# Selected List of Grove Press Drama and Theater Paperbacks

E449    ARDEN, JOHN / Armstrong's Last Goodnight / $1.50

E312    ARDEN, JOHN / Serjeant Musgrave's Dance / $2.45 [See also Modern British Drama, Henry Popkin, ed. GT614 / $5.95]

B109    ARDEN, JOHN / Three Plays: Live Like Pigs, The Waters of Babylon, The Happy Haven / $2.45

E610    ARRABAL, FERNANDO / And They Put Handcuffs on The Flowers / $1.95

E486    ARRABAL, FERNANDO / The Architect and The Emperor of Assyria / $2.40

E611    ARRABAL, FERNANDO / Garden of Delights / $2.95

E521    ARRABAL, FERNANDO / Guernica and Other Plays (The Labyrinth, The Tricycle, Picnic on the Battlefield) / $2.45

E532    ARTAUD, ANTONIN / The Cenci / $1.95

E127    ARTAUD, ANTONIN / The Theater and Its Double (Critical Study) / $2.95

E425    BARAKA, IMAMU AMIRI (LEROI JONES) / The Baptism and The Toilet / $2.45

E471    BECKETT, SAMUEL / Cascando and Other Short Dramatic Pieces (Words and Music, Film, Play, Come and Go, Eh Joe, Endgame) / $1.95

E96    BECKETT, SAMUEL / Endgame / $1.95

E318    BECKETT, SAMUEL / Happy Days / $2.45

E226    BECKETT, SAMUEL / Krapp's Last Tape, plus All That Fall, Embers, Act Without Words I and II / $2.45

E33    BECKETT, SAMUEL / Waiting For Godot / $1.95 [See also Seven Plays of the Modern Theater, Harold Clurman, ed. GT422 / $4.95]

B79    BEHAN, BRENDAN / The Quare Fellow* and The Hostage**: Two Plays / $2.45 *[See also Seven Plays of the Modern Theater, Harold Clurman, ed. GT422 / $4.95] **[See also Modern British Drama, Henry Popkin, ed. GT614 / $5.95]

GT423    BOWERS, FAUBIAN / Theatre in the East: A Survey of Asian Dance and Drama / $3.95

B117    BRECHT, BERTOLT / The Good Woman of Setzuan / $1.95

B80    BRECHT, BERTOLT / The Jewish Wife and Other Short Plays (In Search of Justice, The Informer, The Elephant Calf, The Measures Taken, The Exception and the Rule, Salzburg Dance of Death) / $1.65

B90     BRECHT, BERTOLT / The Mother / $1.45
B108    BRECHT, BERTOLT / Mother Courage and Her
        Children / $1.50
B333    BRECHT, BERTOLT / The Threepenny Opera / $1.45
GT422   CLURMAN, HAROLD (Ed.) / Seven Plays of the Modern
        Theater / $4.95 (Waiting For Godot by Samuel Beckett, The
        Quare Fellow by Brendan Behan, A Taste of Honey by
        Shelagh Delaney, The Connection by Jack Gelber, The
        Balcony by Jean Genet, Rhinoceros by Eugene Ionesco,
        and The Birthday Party by Harold Pinter)
E159    DELANEY, SHELAGH / A Taste of Honey / $1.95 (See also
        Modern British Drama, Henry Popkin, ed., GT614 / $5.95,
        and Seven Plays of the Modern Theater, Harold Clurman,
        ed. GT422 / $4.95)
E402    DURRENMATT, FRIEDRICH / An Angel Comes to Babylon
        and Romulus the Great / $3.95
E628    DURRENMATT, FRIEDRICH / The Meteor / $1.95
E612    DURRENMATT, FRIEDRICH / Play Strindberg / $1.95
E344    DURRENMATT, FRIEDRICH / The Visit / $2.75
B132    GARSON, BARBARA / MacBird! / $1.95
E223    GELBER, JACK / The Connection / $2.45 [See also Seven
        Plays of the Modern Theater, Harold Clurman, ed.
        GT422 / $4.95]
E130    GENET, JEAN / The Balcony / $2.95 [See also Seven Plays
        of the Modern Theater, Harold Clurman, ed. GT422 / $4.95]
E208    GENET, JEAN / The Blacks: A Clown Show / $2.95
E479    GENET, JEAN / Letters to Roger Blin / $1.95
E577    GENET, JEAN / The Maids and Deathwatch:
        Two Plays / $2.95
E374    GENET, JEAN / The Screens / $1.95
E615    HARRISON, PAUL CARTER (Ed.) / The Kuntu
        Drama / $4.95 (Kabnis by Jean Toomer, A Season in the
        Congo by Aime Cesaire, The Owl Answers and A Beast
        Story by Adrienne Kennedy, Great Goodness of Life by
        Imamu Amiri Baraka (LeRoi Jones), Devil Mas' by Lennox
        Brown, The Sty of the Blind Pig by Phillip Hayes Dean, Mars
        By Clay Goss, The Great MacDaddy by Paul Carter
        Harrison)
E457    HERBERT, JOHN / Fortune and Men's Eyes / $2.95

E410    MROZEK, SLAWOMIR / Six Plays: The Police, Out at Sea, Enchanted Night, The Party, Charlie, The Martyrdom of Peter Ohey / $2.45

E433    MROZEK, SLAWOMIR / Tango / $1.95

E462    NICHOLS, PETER / Joe Egg / $2.95

E650    NICHOLS, PETER / The National Health / $3.95

E393    ORTON, JOE / Entertaining Mr. Sloane / $2.95

E470    ORTON, JOE / Loot / $1.95

E567    ORTON, JOE / What The Butler Saw / $2.40

E583    OSBORNE, JOHN / Inadmissible Evidence / $2.45

B110    OSBORNE, JOHN / Plays for England and The World of Paul Slickey / $1.45 (The Blood of the Bambergs and Under Plain Cover)

B354    PINTER, HAROLD / Old Times / $1.95

E315    PINTER, HAROLD / The Birthday Party* and The Room: Two Plays / $1.95 *[See also Seven Plays of the Modern Theater, Harold Clurman, ed. GT422 / $4.95]

E299    PINTER, HAROLD / The Caretaker* and The Dumb Waiter: Two Plays / $1.95 *[See also Modern British Drama, Henry Popkin, ed. GT422 / $5.95]

E411    PINTER, HAROLD / The Homecoming / $1.95

E432    PINTER, HAROLD / The Lover, Tea Party, The Basement: Three Plays / $1.95

E480    PINTER, HAROLD / A Night Out, Night School, Revue Sketches: Early Plays / $1.95

GT614    POPKIN, HENRY (Ed.) / Modern British Drama / $5.95 (A Taste of Honey by Shelagh Delaney, The Hostage by Brendan Behan, Roots by Arnold Wesker, Serjeant Musgrave's Dance by John Arden, One Way Pendulum by N. F. Simpson, The Caretaker by Harold Pinter)

E635    SHEPARD, SAM / The Tooth of Crime and Geography of a Horsedreamer / $3.95

E626    STOPPARD, TOM / Jumpers / $1.95

B319    STOPPARD, TOM / Rosencrantz and Guilderstern Are Dead / $1.95

E660    STOREY, DAVID / In Celebration / $2.95

E62    WALEY, ARTHUR (Translator) / The No Plays of Japan / $3.95

GROVE PRESS, INC., 196 W. Houston St., New York, N.Y. 10014